The Cox Head

Horror

Memoirs from a Parallel Universe™

Universe 98662 X 10^∞

By

Lawrence BoarerPitchford

DEDICATION

Dedicated to those who even now, feel the creeping hand reaching from under the bed - up and under the covers - grasping for your leg in the darkness. Lock your doors, check under the bed, and sleep with the light on. Indrid Cold may pay you a visit this night!

DISCLAIMER

While some of the contents of this novel reflect historical characters, relationships, and events, any resemblance to your universe is purely coincidental. The story and events are purely the construct of the author.

.

CONTENTS

ACKNOWLEDGMENTS

Senior Editor ~ Wendy Schirmer

Copy Editor ~ Roselyn Pitchford

Cover Art ~ Boarerpitchford.com

CHAPTER 1
HELL'S GATEWAY

Excerpt from the last entry in the diary of ~ William Flannery, M.D, PhD

The black oily brackish water consumes me. It rises above my ankles now and fills me like a stinking tide of foulness. In the middle of the chamber, there echoes my own voice speaking to me in transit prose. My thoughts - bruising my mind. Beyond my tenacious clinging to sanity, I now hear the voices both day and night. They chip away at my conscience with vicious and malicious intent. It licks at my feet, crawls up my bones – it is eating the very marrow of my soul.

I'll travel to the cave one more time, but I am not sure that I will be able to stop the inevitable before my soul is agonized beyond reason. I cannot stop the machine now. If this be the last of my notes, and you find it – shut the cover and burn this codex. The evil is already among you. Your world is now different than mine. Do not let curiosity lead you to the cave, for ruin lies there. Trust me, for I have nothing to gain from falsehood now. When your eyes stray behind the veil, you will fall within, then there is no coming back.

I close now. I leave my wedding ring, money clip, diamond stickpin, and any hope of salvation in this small wooden box. If I return – I may not be human any longer. If I don't, you may not be human any longer. I pray it is not the latter – for if I am the sacrifice to end this horror – it will be enough for humanity.

May 28, 1918 Battle of Cantigny

Smoke lurked across the landscape, moving like a serpent born of fire. It slithered amongst the dead and dying, stopping only long enough to consume souls in a voracious and unending fervor.

Jack rubbed his eyes, clearing away the dripping slurry of mud on his face. A sound like a church bell echoed in his head. With the back of his sleeve, he brushed the blood from his cheeks. All around - arms and legs, heads and chunks of pale meat lay jumbled and mixed into the black earth. The ripe stench of putrefaction and gunpowder added to the visage – that of the desolation in hell.

The world began to spin, and Jack nearly fell - catching himself by driving the butt of his rifle into the ground. He looked up to see a tangle of barbed wire inches away from his eye.

For a moment, he thought of Alighieri's Divine Comedy – in every direction he looked, lay a rhapsodic lament of that madness.

Jack's eyes focused ahead. Miles of tortured ground lain covered in tan and blue uniforms - many draped along, and tangled within, the endless coils of barbed wire. Blood filled puddles, and dismembered limbs of both man and beast protruded from the earth.

The ground shook, and from the gray sky, mud and rocks rained down. Jack took half a dozen steps, his mind fuzzy as if it too were cloaked by that relentless shifting fog that moved all around. There was a flash in the distance. Shortly after, came the report of artillery fire.

The ground shook, and more dirt fell all about– blood, bile, meat, and clods of dark mud. A thick veil of white passed. In the shifting clumps of smoke, the shadowed image of a screaming face took shape, then stretched, and finally swirled into nothing but more haze.

Something grasped his legging. Whatever it was, it was not letting go. In the blinding haze, he reached down. Something sticky and wet clung to his pants.

Whatever it was, it remained attached to his gator. Reaching down, he pulled it up. In his hand - a disembodied forearm, the tendons, veins, and ligaments hanging down.

The fingers contracted into a fist, then flexed several times. He dropped it - shock hit him like a lightning bolt.

Jack turned to vomit – but then came the relentless stinking mist. In the distance, the tat-tat-tat sound of machine gunfire erupted. Voices were there too - cries of men, the screams of horses. Small arms fire came from some faraway place.

He staggered forward and fell into a muddy trench. A sound like a steam whistle erupted in his ears, and dirt fell in on him. He rolled to the side. The battle came into clear audible focus.

Men were screaming, explosive shells were hitting all around and bursting overhead. The veil in his mind was thinning, and the reality of where he was hit him between the eyes.

German, French, and English commands flew from every direction. In his hand was his Springfield thirty-caliber rifle with the bayonet dripping blood.

Raising his hand to his face, he wiped away something wet. He stood and looked at his muddy hand. The brown dirt was intermixed with strings of dark red - he didn't know if it was his or someone else's blood.

Boots were smashing into puddled water. They were coming down the trench toward him. The smoke – the mist – like a curtain swallowed him.

From where? Left? Right?

He turned his rife to the left and put the butt into the crook of his thigh - something spit itself on the end of his bayonet. The fog thinned. The red cheeks of a man his age stared back at him.

Opening his mouth, the man said something in German, then Jack watched as his eyes changed from slate blue to dull gray.

He withdrew his bayonet with a jerk, then stepped back, putting his foot into something slick. Looking down, he saw his leg extending from the ripped body cavity of a torso - no head, no arms, and no legs.

Pulling his foot out, he moved down the dark brown ditch. In the distance, he heard a whistle blowing - more machine gun fire - more artillery. In the din, the screams outmatched the screeching of the shells as they rained down.

He knew, just over that dirt-lip were unleashed human-made mechanical horrors that devoured both men and beast. He shook his head to clear it. A skull-cracking headache began to form.

Turning a corner, he saw an American soldier sitting in the mud. From both, his hands hung down his intestines like sausages hanging in a deli. He was trying to keep them from lying in the dirty water. Rats feasted upon his flesh, then scattered into the filthy bloody muck.

"I seem to have dropped my pouch," the young man said to Jack. "I can't find it. The Sergeant is going to yell at me if I can't find it!" There was pure panic in his voice.

A rat came from within the boy's torn flesh and ran past Jack.

Blinding light, hot air, and hissing shrapnel tore into the trench walls. Thrown into the mist, Jack rolled to a stop against an iron rod tipped with torn barbed wire. His mind was rattled, and he got onto his elbows and knees. His rifle was missing.

Groping for his pistol, he noted it was gone too. His pants were down around his knees, and he struggled to get to his feet. Blood was coming from his nose and ears.

Jack heard the bolt of a rifle locking into position. The white mist cleared again.

Standing with his back to Jack was a German wearing a pickle helmet – the man's rifle raised, and all his attention bore down to an unseen victim.

Jack pulled up his pants, cinched his belt, then removed his knuckleduster knife. He crouched, then leapt, ramming the blade into the man's back.

The soldier gasped, then struggled. The Hun's body jerked as his limbs flailed. A pleading whimper escaped the man's lips, then he was limp and silent.

Jack lay the man into the dirt and withdrew his knife, sheathing the weapon. He grabbed the enemy's mouser and checked to see if it was loaded. It was. He took the man's ammunition belt and moved forward.

His mind was distant. He felt he was looking down upon his body, walking like a zombie through the horror. Somewhere, far away, his inner monologue called out to him. "None of this is real. You'll wake up in your bed and be at home." Then, Jack felt something - eyes upon him - clammy and wet perspiration poured from his face and body.

He turned with a jerk. The smothering haze vanished in a gust of wind. There, extending to hell's horizon, were soldiers – their pale features as white as snow. They stared at him – their faces expressing confusion – their eyes bore into his as if shocked to see him in this landscape. The one closest to him opened his mouth and gave a shrill scream.

Over Jack's shoulder echoed a voice in his ears. "Al mawat al alam."

Those thousands of spectral soldiers began to fade, blown away by an unseen wind. In an instant, there were none to be seen, and only the crawling sensation of horror leaping up and down Jack's spine remained.

A swath of dirty yellow mist came, and Jack began to choke and cough. He went down on one knee – groping for his gas mask. A shock ran through his body as a circular hole formed. Beyond - a clear sky evolved from the drifting smoke.

Palm trees waved in that sky, as tan sand yawned away to the horizon. A man bare-chested and without pants or a weapon sat on the banks of a flowing river surrounded by grass and flowers.

Jack got to his feet. The man also stood – his face was not human – the face of a wild dog glared at him.

"Al mawat al alam!" it spoke.

Jack was consumed – fire was about him, his skin was burning, his eyes felt as though they would burst. He jerked wildly, clawing at his throat – then came darkness that swallowed his mind and his soul.

CHAPTER 2
BUREAU BUSINESS

Director William J. Flynn sat opposite Treasury Agent Jack Parlance. The polished birch table separated the two men only by a few feet.

"An anarchist breaks into your home. He rapes your wife, and you capture him before he escapes. What do you do?" Flynn asked.

Jack pulled out a Black Cat cigarette and put it into his mouth. He narrowed his eyes as he fished around in the side pocket of his tweed jacket. Pulling out a brass Bower lighter, he stroked the flint, hid the flame in his hands, and filled his lungs with the healing power of tobacco smoke. He looked across the table, then exhaled as he spoke.

"I'd arrest the son-of-a-bitch and bring him in. Then, I'd watch him jerk about at the end of a rope, then I'd piss on his grave."

The corner of Flynn's mouth turned up, and he nodded his head. "A valid answer. I admire your restraint."

"It helps that I'm not married," Jack replied.

"So, about the offer. It is on the table, Agent Parlance. You can leave the Treasury and come over to the Bureau or stay where you're at. As you know, we're growing fast and will have lots of space for advancement. We can use experienced agents like you to enforce all these new federal laws. Washington will keep churning them out – you can bet on it!"

Jack took another drag from his cigarette. "Sounds like a place a man can grow his career." The gray smoke spewed out of Jack's mouth with each word. "I don't mind busting a few jaws and enforcing a few federal laws."

"Good. Go down the hall to the administration office. They'll have you fill out the paperwork. Then, go down to the armory and pick out some weapons. I'm sure you used some of them in the war."

Jack nodded. "I'm quite familiar with the use of

firearms."

Flynn put a folder in front of Jack and nodded toward the door. "Here's your first assignment. Some rich kid vanished. He's a libertine – probably drank himself to death. But we've been asked to find out what happened to him. You're free to use any means at your disposal to get to the bottom of this. Report back to me only. You're dismissed," he curtly stated.

Parlance stood up, dwarfing the Bureau Chief and his desk. Flynn looked up at the hulking man and added. "Parlance, you're going to scare the hell out of them yeggs, commies, and spies." He looked back down at his paperwork and grabbed an ink pen from the well on his blotter pad. "We'll talk more soon," he said as he motioned with his hand for Jack to exit.

* * *

Jack carried the weapons and a box of paperwork down to his black Ford Model T. When he was a kid, automobiles were just a rare curiosity. Now those combustion driven wagons were everywhere.

The hour was late, and the night consumed the blocks of state buildings and roads. He looked down the street. Most of the streetlights were lit – bathing the sidewalk with a dull orange glow. Beyond - the oppressive darkness was all about.

He surveyed the vacant street. At night, the streets of D.C. were mostly empty, roamed by specters and ghosts from the city's illustrious past - blanketed in shadow – save for the occasional row of streetlamps around the center of town.

He loaded his items into the back seat. Going to the driver's side, he opened the door, pushed the ignition-switch closed. After pulling the throttle lever in and out a few times, he went to the front and cranked the engine.

One crank – the vehicle backfired, and dark smoke filled the air. Second crank – the car rattled to life. He climbed into the cab. The vehicle sank as the springs compressed. Taking the throttle lever, the car rolled ahead over the cobbled street.

He turned right onto New York Avenue and made a right onto Florida. A streetlight illuminated his destination.

He pulled over to the side at 979 Florida Avenue and let the Ford rattle to a halt. Applying the hand brake, the engine sputtered, backfired twice, then stopped.

The block where he lived was oddly shaped - an isosceles triangle with its longest sides along Florida Ave. He stepped out. The car rocked as the springs groaned. The chassis rose to its standard height from the road.

He took out his equipment, went up the stairs to the mahogany door, inserted his key, and went inside.

The Seth Thomas clock on the wall was ticking. Stale air and dust, with just the hint of mildew, filled his nose. He approached the avocado green couch and set down his bundle. Next to it, he put the Thompson and shotgun, took off his shoulder holster, and put the pistol on the end-table. Walking to the center of the room, he reached up, turned the valve to 'open', and ignited the gas with his lighter. His small home had yet to be fitted with electricity.

Afterward, he took out the pack of Black Cat's and tapped one out of the box. Taking it between his lips, he lit it with the still burning lighter.

The room was now awash with the dim-orange glow of the gaslight. In the kitchen, he lit the lamp, and in the bedroom, he did the same. As he turned, a pair of eyes watched him from the closet. He crouched down.

"There you are, Mr. Pinkerton," he said. "What have you been up to all day? Making sure the Confederates stay at bay?"

The gray and black cat emerged from the closet and stretched forward, elongating its body and sticking its butt and tail into the air. A muted meow bubbled from the creature, then it came to Jack and rubbed several times along his hand, then on his brown trousers.

"I got something I think you'll like," Jack said as he

went to the kitchen and took down a can of tuna.

Opening the container, he dumped the contents onto a small saucer and put it by the door-jam.

"Eat up, you shaggy puss," he added.

Mister Pinkerton approached the dish, sniffed it a few times, looked up at Jack, then back down, and started eating.

Turning back to the icebox, Jack opened it and looked inside - a bottle of milk - fresh from the morning, a bar of butter, and a bottle of half-empty Cambus whiskey. Taking the whiskey, he found a tumbler and put it on the table.

He poured a half glass, sat down, and drank it slowly.

"Ya love yer fish, Mr. Pinkerton, and that's all well and good, but a man loves his whiskey, and no namby-pamby cock sucking bastards up on The Hill can make it otherwise," he said.

The cat finished eating. He ran his tongue along the outside of his mouth several times, then began licking his paw and rubbing his muzzle.

Jack looked around the room; icebox, cupboards, several shelves, and a gas oven - seldom used. Much better than the squalor he lived in as a child. At the least, there was no screaming, no nightly violence - angry words from drunken parents, and no blood on the floor to clean up.

He stood up and went to one of the shelves. On it sat two cans of corn, a jar of peaches, a tin of sardines, and a package of saltine crackers. He took down the sardines and crackers and put them on the table. "Well, Pinkerton, old son, looks like we're both having fish tonight." He opened the tin and crackers and ate.

Once finished, he took the bottle of whiskey and went into the living room. Sitting on the couch, he shoved the boxes to the side and took out the folder marked Bureau Use Only. He opened the folder and read the first document.

Assignment 0001267; Jack Parlance, investigating agent. Investigate the disappearance of Jody Dobs. Last known residence Central Park West and West 63rd Street apartment 1100, Manhattan, New York. Priority: High. Report all findings to the Bureau Chief only. Determine if foul play is involved.

The second typed document was behind the assignment sheet. It was a thin trace-paper letter dated 1905 with a faded red stamp – 'Department of War' across the top.

Dear Doctor Blake,

Your talents have come to my attention, and now I write you to see if you will join me at my residence to discover the remedies for certain forms of madness. Those of us alienists who study the mind know that within are powers undreamt of by the laymen.

Inside that gray organ lies the ability to define man's history and create one's destiny. I feel that you know this too, based on your recent publication, The Curative Power of the Human Mind. I have read this treatise and think that you and I could do much good work together.

If you would be so kind as to join me on November twenty-second in my home at Gray Manor on Cox Head Point, in Maine, I will make clear to you my focus and efforts. I shall send a carriage to retrieve you from the train station at Ashdale. Expect a two-week engagement, at the end of which I shall ask you to join my work. I trust you will be discrete, in that you will bring only yourself.

I look forward to our discussions and exploration of the human intellect. God speed you, and safe journey.

Regards,
Doctor, Hans Frauhafer, Ph.D., M.D.

Jack set the letter aside, then took up the Bureau's report on Frauhafer. He looked it over and noted the word anarchists mentioned in several places. He put that aside and took up a photo of the man from 1899.

Frauhafer was tall and wearing a fashionable black formal jacket like the ones so popular in the late Nineteenth Century.

His face was weathered and wrinkled, and his nose long and pointy. A thick black beard hung down to his chest, and his head was capped with a tall top-hat.

He put the picture aside. Next, he pulled out a dossier with black letters on the cover; Psychiatrist Doctor Frauhafer arrives in Bagdad with team of Antiquarians, 1902. Objective unknown. British concerned over whispers of satanic rights and missing persons.

Next, he took out a clipping from the Washington Bee newspaper circa 1920. A bizarre story unfolded.

A local constable was approached by a Catholic priest. The priest was worried that several local hobos who had come to his church for free meals had stopped coming.

The weather was turning cold, and he wanted to make sure the men were not freezing to death out in the elements. The officer made a concerted effort to locate the men but did not find them.

A month later, three corpses turned up near a hobo camp on the outskirts of the town. The bodies were recently dismembered. The coroner first speculated that the dead men were on the railroad tracks near the rail yard and most likely hit by a train. However, the doctor who did the autopsy found they had been dismembered at the joints with surgical precision.

Hans Frauhafer, Ph.D., M.D., suddenly inserted himself into the investigation and stated that "The missing men were dismembered by a butcher or physician - and the bodies dumped at the rail yard."

Jack turned over the document, and in red ink, the words Why Frauhafer? was scrawled.

"Yes – why a psychiatrist, Pinkerton old fella?" he said, and then petted the cat.

He pulled out another folder and read the label. "Spiritualists and the Occult."

Half a dozen index cards with names and addresses were inside, along with a four-page document listing stolen Egyptian relics, macabre meetings, and several well-known people of blue-blood pedigree from Manhattan – Jody Dobbs included.

As he flipped to the last page, Frauhafer's name appeared again, this time with the label Odd Goings-On in Maine above. Jack took up his glass and, in one draft, consumed the whiskey.

Setting the glass down, he reached into the box and pulled out some pictures of round stone disks with odd markings on them. "Book of the Dead?" Jack read aloud.

Notes on several murdered women and two mug shots of rough-looking fellows came out of the box, followed by three more folders.

He opened another folder. Xavier Blake, Ph.D., M.D., a professor of psychiatry teaching at Georgetown University and practicing at an asylum in New York.

Blake had come to the United States from Prussia in 1883, already a doctor in the field of the mind.

He made a practice in New York on the island of Manhattan and was suspected of belonging to a secret society called the 'Timber Framers.' Later, however, that evidence was lost in a fire – according to the official notation.

In 1915, he was suspected and charged with botching a lobotomy at the Ward's Island Asylum, but he was exonerated of the charges a few months later when he gave evidence against Frauhafer about unethical experiments. His address was listed on an index card with the man's schedule of hospital rounds, and times of which he could be found at his home on the island. Jack put the dossier aside.

The next packet was titled 'McFadden and Company'. He opened it and was pleasantly surprised to see several photos of a beautiful young woman in a party dress.

"Pinkerton, old man, I think we've hit the jackpot," he

said. He examined it closely, then held it at arms-reach. "Not bad gams if I do say so myself."

Putting the pictures aside, he began to read the report: A young socialite named Brenda McFadden, whose father lost nearly all the family's wealth in the depression of 1883. To make ends meet, her father opened a few breweries and distilleries around the country. Over twenty-six years, he nearly made back all his lost fortune...until the Volstead Act.

Gary McFadden committed suicide on October 22, 1920, as all his businesses were closed. His wife died several months later of consumption at a Staten Island infirmary. Brenda, his loving daughter, moved to Manhattan around 1920, where she bought an apartment on Forty-second Avenue.

A Treasury Agent was assigned to determine where her money was coming from and concluded after a year's investigation that she had no verifiable income. A document dated a year later revealed that she owned fifty speakeasies around New York and twice as many in Chicago. She was linked to prostitution, gambling, and bootlegging. Her criminal empire was large, but no charges were ever levied.

A postscript stated she was acquainted with Xavier Blake, the doctor who'd treated McFadden after he was removed from Frauhafer's care in July 1920, and sent to Blake's practice shortly before his suicide. On the back was an address of a gin-joint she frequented, and the times she could be found there.

Jack reached into the box and withdrew another manila folder. The documents covered the movements and acquaintances of a low-level thug named Jimmy "Blue Eyes" McKerry.

Jimmy was described as a handsome fellow who rose through the ranks of the Irish Kilkerny gang and ran numbers, prostitution, booze, and drugs on the west side of Manhattan. As Jack read down the page, he noted that the researcher cross-referenced Jimmy with Brenda McFadden. It appeared she was employing Jimmy as a bodyguard and muscle to help manage her speakeasies. An index card with Jimmy's movements was attached.

Jack sat back and put his feet up on the coffee table. He poured himself another glass of whiskey, held the glass on his knee, and drew in the acrid smoke from his cigarette. Mr. Pinkerton mewed, and Jack looked over at the clock.

"Time we hit the hay, old boy," he said as he exhaled the gray cloud into the room. "Lots to do upon the 'morrow."

CHAPTER 3
THE SEARCHER

Jack sat up and silenced the loud bells on the clock. Popping a Black Cat into his mouth, he lit it, bringing the end to a bright cherry glow. In the flicker of the lighter's flame, the clock read 4:00 a.m.

He got up and went to the bathroom, brushed his teeth, shaved, then splashed some cologne across his face and chest.

After flushing the toilet, he moved to the kitchen, made some toast and black coffee, and then went into the living room.

Putting on his shoulder holster, he ate his breakfast, sipped his coffee, then put out some dry cat food in a bowl. Taking up his travel satchel and the Jody Dobbs folder, he made for the door.

"Ms. Hastings will be looking in on you while I'm gone. Watch the house! Don't let the Johnny-Rebs in," he said to Mr. Pinkerton as he closed the door.

The tin-Lizzy popped and sputtered as he drew out the throttle and adjusted the spark. It didn't take long to arrive at 50 Massachusetts Ave NE. The tremendous and looming edifice of Union Station was a massive affair. Three grand archways led into the largest room in the world – The Concourse.

Jack found parking and went into the station and bought a ticket to Manhattan. An hour wait at the station and four hours on the train meant a long journey for a day's work.

The powerful steam engine lurched forward, dragging the half-mile long chain of passenger cars out of the station. Jack sat on the right side, facing forward, in the middle of the car. He rubbed his hand along the seat lined with a coarse black and red checkered patterned cloth. Jack leaned up against the window, tilted his hat forward to cover his eyes.

Hey, Jack… you awake yet? The rats – they're eating your feet. Better stop em before they get to your balls!" Someone poked Jack in the chest.

Jack opened his eyes and looked up into the exposed sinus cavity and empty eye sockets of a young man wearing a Doughboy uniform and helmet.

"Mike…" Jack said with shock.

Jack's eyes flew open. The electric lights were on, and the sky outside was gray and threatening rain. He sat forward and pulled out a Black Cat, put it in his mouth with a shaking hand, and lit it with his lighter. He looked around. The car was half full of travelers.

Taking his leather satchel, he stood up and made for the dining car. As he walked, he drew in the pungent smoke.

He passed through one car, then another. The dining car was brightly lit. Rain began hitting the side of the train. Square tables lined the walls – white tablecloths, bone-china cups, and polished silverware complemented the setting. Jack sat down.

"What can I get for you, sir?" a young black man dressed in all white asked.

"Bring me a scotch and toast," Jack said.

"Sir, we don't carry liquor on the train – it's illegal these days," the young porter said.

Jack solemnly nodded. "Right… right, you are. Bring me a cup of strong coffee – black – and the toast."

The young man nodded and headed down the aisle toward the kitchen car. Jack looked out the window at the passing countryside.

Farms and pasture lands moved by at a swift pace. He'd taken a similar path many years before, ordered to report to the Brooklyn docks to ship out to England – then from there to France. In France, it was the same -

travel by train to the front. All along the way, he thought – If this is my experience in this war, I'm a lucky man. He soon found out he was not that lucky.

Jack looked over at two women sitting at one of the tables. Neither noticed him. He looked back out the window. From time to time, they passed through a town or city.

Baltimore was fading into the background as Newark fast approached. Next would come Trenton, then Grand Central Terminal.

The porter brought his order, then retreated to the service bar at the back of the car. Jack drank his coffee – taking bites from his buttered toast and looking out the window. For a moment, somewhere off in the distance, he thought he heard artillery. At a crossroads, a group of men in khaki-colored Doughboy uniforms watched the train pass by.

Jack shook his head – the men were gone – just empty road remained. He fished a small silver flask from his jacket, took a swig, and then poured a little into his half-filled coffee cup. Another cigarette was smoked. When would the war end – when would the memories of that experience stop? Smokes and booze would have to help him until those horrors faded in his memory.

He put his satchel on the table and pulled out the folder about Jody Dobbs. He was the youngest son of William Henry Dobbs, one of the richest men in New York. The young man was a socialite, raised with a silver spoon in his mouth and wanting for nothing, except maybe attention and love.

Dobbs' mother rarely saw her six children -- all raised by governesses, educated by tutors, and sent to wallow in the Manhattan clubs and penthouses. Jody vanished a year previously. Documents indicated that he became a hedonist – frequenting sadomasochist clubs, homosexual bars, private bohemian gin-joints, and several spiritual cults located in Manhattan, New Jersey, and the Bronx.

The local cops were unclear on exactly when he disappeared. A maid reported him missing when she failed to see him at the end of a month. A few wealthy friends also came forward – but none could pinpoint the day Dobbs became a missing person.

Down along the margins, the investigator wrote that Doctor Frauhafer was treating the man for his homosexual proclivities but stopped when William Dobbs withdrew his financial commitment to support Frauhafer's latest asylum project. Somewhere within the following six weeks – Jody Dobbs slipped away.

The train shook as the cars took a turn in the tracks. Jack looked down into the oily black abyss of his coffee as the liquid swayed from side to side. He finished his toast and wiped his hands on the white linen napkin. Catching the porter's attention, he motioned for him to bring more coffee. Within the blink of an eye, the young man came with a stainless-steel coffee pot and poured more into Jack's cup.

Checking his watch, Jack scooted his chair back, then took out an artist drawn image of a medallion. It had a crystal at the top and strange hieroglyphs along the sides. In the middle was the image of the dog-faced god Anubis.

Jack took a long drag from his cigarette, then blew out the smoke from the corner of his mouth. Up came the coffee cup, and he took a mouthful.

Next to the image was written, 'Missing from American Museum of Natural History in New York 1917.' He flipped the page over. On the back were two columns. In one, a description of an Anubis headdress found in the possession of a man named Filbert Hollins – an associate of Dr. Frauhafer. The man was arrested. Under interrogation, he stated that he was the manager of an Egyptian enthusiast club, and his purpose was to hold open the doors to the underworld. The author wrote – 'Completely out of his mind'.

In the other column, a description of several missing

young women. Two chorus girls and two girls from a local boarding house had vanished.

"Thirty minutes to the station!" called the conductor as he came through the car. "Thirty minutes – to the station!"

Jack had another cup of coffee and smoke, then picked up his papers and satchel and headed back to the coach car.

The cars rattled to a halt. The porters and conductors came and went, then opened the doors to let the passengers off and onto the concourse. Satchel in hand, Jack stepped off the ladder and headed toward the vast open space that was Grand Central Station.

Once through the marble-floored atrium and past the giant clock, he made his way to the exit and out into the bustle of Manhattan Island.

Hailing a cab, he instructed the driver to take him to 201 West 79th Street, the Lucerne Hotel on the Upper West Side.

The ride was comfortable, and Jack watched the pedestrians along the sidewalks coming and going. He paid the cabbie and then went into the rectangular multistory red-façade building.

An older man stood at the desk. "Can I help you?" he asked as Jack approached.

Jack handed over a postcard. "I have a reservation for five nights."

"I see you received our confirmation postie. Works like a charm – for all our preferred guests. Five days will come to ten dollars."

Jack produced his wallet and took out a ten-dollar bill. "I may get messages via telegram or telephone. Make sure that I get them."

The man handed Jack a key and rang a bell. A negro bellhop rushed over.

"Any bags, sir?"

Jack shook his head. "Just what I'm carrying."

The young man took the key from Jack. "I'll show you to your room, sir."

Jack had chosen the Lucerne Hotel for its location – he'd had no idea it was a posh place. The gold gilding and scrollwork, the marble floors, the brass and chrome fixtures fitted with emerald-green glass – it felt like a palace. He was impressed.

On the third floor, he followed the bellhop to room 341. The young man unlocked the door, and Jack gave him a quarter for his trouble.

"Thank you, sir! If there is anything else, please call down to the reception desk and ask for Clarence."

Jack grunted an affirmation and then went into his room, closing the door behind him.

Laying down on the bed, Jack checked his watch. It was now 1:00 pm. He was a bit hungry. Sitting up, he grabbed the dossier of the Dobbs boy, put it into his inside jacket pocket, and headed for the door.

He exited the building onto 79th Street and wandered for a while until he found a diner on Columbus Avenue. The food was good, and the portions ample.

After eating, he looked at the address of his quarry - Central Park West and West 63rd Street apartment 1100. He paid the fifty cents for his meal, left two bits on the table, and exited. Hailing a cab, he gave the driver the address. Less than ten minutes later, he was standing in front of the tan stone and brick building.

Jack showed his credentials to the doorman. The man directed Jack to the building manager.

"Come on and follow me," the manager said. "They still own the loft." The manager got into the elevator. He instructed the lift operator to take them to the proper floor.

The operator stopped the lift, and Jack and the manager got out.

"That boy was one queer fellow," the manager stated.

"Was?" Jack asked. "Why did you use that word?"

The manager looked surprised. "I assumed he's dead. At least no one has seen him in almost a year."

Jack eyed the manager for a moment, then grunted and turned down a broad hall paved with dark orange metallic tiles. Along the passage were four fixtures – two per side. Two by the lift were polished brass with blue molded glass fitted into it like sapphire flames. The two nearest the apartment door were reflective chrome with dark red glass similarly fashioned.

The manager stopped at the double white doors and inserted his key. Opening the portal, he stood to the side.

"Would you like me to come in with you?" the manager asked.

Jack looked down at the man with a look of annoyance. "No. Leave me the key, and you can go. I'll drop it off as I leave."

Nodding, the manager turned and went back to the elevator, rang for the lift, then looked back at the doorway. "He was a strange one that kid," he said as the elevator arrived. "Lots of odd comings and goings out of that door." The manager entered the lift and was gone.

CHAPTER 4
UNCOMFORTABLE DISCOVERY

Jack entered Jody's residence. He closed the door behind him and locked it. The first thing he noticed as he entered loft 1100 was the strong scent of frankincense in the air. It hung in the large open entry like a perfume one might find in a harem born of some exotic Persian fantasy tale.

From his vantage, Jack was struck by how the walls were placed... they were erected like drama sets. None connected to the high open roof or blocked the light cascading through the windows.

Looking down, he noted a golden stripe painted on the floor. He began walking along the line almost out of impulse.

Spacious was an understatement. The entire floor was broken up by those odd walls placed to create a sense of separation between living space, kitchen, parlor, study, and bedroom.

As he reached the far end, he found a door built into an actual room. It was locked, making the enclosed area beyond inaccessible. The apartment key did not fit this lock, so Jack cocked back his leg and kicked in the door.

He reached around the edge of the door into the dark void and groped for the electric pushbutton-switch to turn on the electric light. A click echoed into the room. Several bright bulbs flared into existence. Jack stood, stunned.

He'd read about the Inquisition and the torture of Jesus as written in the New Testament – but he was unprepared to see the implements laid out and hanging upon the wall before him.

"Son-of-a-bitch," Jack whispered into the cool air.

He checked the door on either side – the room appeared devoid of life. He entered. Leather aprons, cords of steel and leather were attached to tables. On the wall were shackles and collars attached to chains. Chrome pliers, clamps, and probes were set out on metallic trays and tables—a vast array of phallic objects.

Jack walked around, being careful not to disturb anything. There appeared to be no blood or sign of murder. The dust on the objects indicated no one had used them recently.

He came back out and went through every drawer and scrap of paper in the apartment. Searching the area by the phone, he found an introduction card – white with black lettering. On it was printed a time and an address. Jack took it. The location was not far.

A black notebook caught Jack's attention, and he opened it. It was an appointment book. He flipped to the last entry – 'I'll enjoy the Virgin for a while. Hope I don't burn. July 9th, Maine 10:40 a.m.'. The date printed on the appointment page was June 1921. No other notations were present.

He finished his search, then made for the elevator and the lobby. Only the sound of the whirling pulleys and electric motor filled the lift as it descended. Jack was silent with his thoughts. Once outside, he hailed a cab.

The cabbie dropped him off at an old three-story Victorian house with a for sale sign at the door. Jack tried the doorknob and found it locked. He looked around – no one was watching – he forced it open with his shoulder.

Closing the door, he looked around. The afternoon light was coming through the gaps in the curtains in golden shafts. He pushed in the light switch, and nothing happened. No power.

Going from room to room, he found the place empty on all three floors. Finally, he came to the basement door. He opened it, took out his lighter, ignited it, and held it aloft as he descended the stairs into the musty-smelling darkness.

Shimmering shadows flashed and wavered against the railing. Pipes and black rubber-coated wires were suspended from the wooden joists. There was dampness down there. He moved toward the far wall.

A cold shiver ran up Jack's spine. To his right was an interior wall made of lath and plaster. To his left was a cement foundation wall met in the middle by a redbrick retaining wall holding back dark, damp earth.

A rat squeaked and dashed into a drainage pipe. There, a figure crouched in the darkness.

Jack drew his pistol. "You – stand up and show me your hands!"

The person remained hunkered down. Jack took a step – and the individual began to rise. To Jack's horror – it had no feet – the thing was connected to the ground by a fuzzy gray tendril of mist.

It turned. Jack backed up against the plaster wall. The face was gaunt and ashen. There was a terrible cry of anguish. The thing flew at Jack and passed through him. Cold sweat poured from his pores. The lighter fell. Darkness swallowed him.

He crouched and quickly searched with his hand for the Bower. His hand touched something – a shoe… someone was standing in front of him in the black.

Recoiling, he again hit up against the plaster wall. There was a cracking sound. He groped along the cement floor. His hand landed on the lighter. Flicking the flint, the room was again bathed in the dim orange glow. There was no one else there.

Jack looked around, frantic. As he moved, the wall behind him groaned, then fell away. The broken part collapsed, and in the dusty dim light, he saw the dried mummified corpse of a person chained to a brick wall.

Jack stood outside the building, waiting for nearly twenty minutes. The police asked him to stay near while they did their preliminary evaluation of the property. Jack just waited and watched.

Don Hurston, the police detective, came out of the house. "Agent Parlance," he called. "Don't know who the stiff is, but he… or she's been there for a while. The coroner will take a look. We had to break the wrists to get the shackles off it – they were fastened with rivets. Most likely driven into place with a hammer and anvil. Looks pretty old."

The gray smoke streamed out of Jack's mouth as he thought about this. "The clothes look recent."

"I guess they do. All the body had on was this –" Hurston handed Jack a yellowed folded piece of paper. "We'll know more once we get the body down to the morgue. You want to ride along?" the detective asked.

"Sure," Jack replied as he lit his lighter and examined the paper. It was the size of a postcard – but thin like regular paper – yellow with age. "Looks like this is a document from a place called The Mercantile Meat Processing Plant – in Pennsylvania. Say's something about the invoice for SFB paid in full and provides a phone number to call for pickup of meat."

"I'll need that back," Hurston said. "Come on, the ambulance lads are bringing the body out now."

"I'll need the autopsy report as soon as possible," Jack stated.

Hurston looked at Jack sideways. "I might suggest a bit more decorum, Agent Parlance – remember you have no jurisdiction here. Consider my assistance a courtesy – one law enforcement officer to another."

Jack cracked a smile. "I'll do that."

The ride down to the hospital was not long, and Jack explained why he was at the house. He pulled out a Back Cat and offered one to Hurston.

"Thanks – but I'm a pipe man myself." Hurston pulled out a maple pipe from his lapel pocket and put it into his mouth. Retrieving a match, Hurston struck it on the dashboard and lit his pipe – filling the cab with the rich smelling scent of pipe tobacco.

"Not a lot of crime in this area. Mostly posh and old

Bluebloods around here," Hurston said.

"It's a Blueblood I'm looking for," Jack replied.

"Anyone I might know?" Hurston asked.

"Jody Dobbs," Jack said.

"About a year ago? No ransom note, and no leads – we still have the case open," Hurston stated. "If you find out anything – let me know."

"One courtesy for another," Jack mumbled as he exhaled a column of gray smoke out the window.

Hurston chuckled. "Something like that."

Once at the hospital, they followed the body down into the basement and the morgue. A thin fellow wearing a stained smock with a cigarette between his fingers waited.

"Doctor Lipton, this is Agent Jack Parlance from Washington, D.C. Please show him all the respect you show us," Hurston stated.

"I don't show you bully-boys any respect," Lipton replied.

Hurston chuckled. "You're in good hands here," he said to Jack.

Lipton walked over as the remains were placed on the stainless-steel table. The sheet was removed, and the doctor solemnly nodded his head.

"Where are the hands?" Lipton asked.

"There under the body," said one of the ambulance drivers.

Lipton again nodded and then turned on a bright light over the table. "Thanks, boys. You can go. This stiff's in good hands now -" He stopped abruptly then laughed. "No pun and all that," he stated. "If you want, Agent Parlance, you can stand here and watch me, or you can head out and grab something to eat or drink. Should take me a couple of hours to get some answers for you." He took up a scalpel.

"Okay – I'll be back," Jack said as he headed for the door.

Lipton put the cigarette into the corner of his mouth.

"The old Park Avenue Tavern is not far down the street. It's a restaurant now – Italian food, I think. I understand that if you tell the waiter that Hoover sent you, they'll give you the cocktail menu."

Jack nodded. "You do know that I'm an agent of the government, right?"

Lipton chuckled. "You don't look like the type to turn away a glass of scotch."

Jack removed his silver flask, opened it, took a drink, and then handed it to Lipton.

Lipton smiled and took it – swallowed several gulps, then handed it back. "I'm a rather good judge of people. Though – I'm usually meeting them after they've expired."

Jack chuckled, shook his head, turned, and again headed for the door.

Jack paid thirty-five cents for his dinner. Expensive, he thought. Now he was back on the street. Making his way back to the hospital, Jack observed the many inhabitants of the city. On this side of town, they were mostly well dressed, as if coming or going to a soiree or attending the theater. A few, dressed like the working class, wandered the streets gazing into the glass-framed shops.

Ahead was the hospital. He was almost there.

Stopping at one of the shops, he peered into the window. Across the street, a black Hudson had pulled over. The vehicle windows were odd – they appeared to be mirrored. He watched the car for some time.

Jack made a mental note of its shape and model, then continued to the hospital again. The strange car remained on the street. As Jack approached the hospital, he looked over his shoulder, and the car was gone.

"What do you have for me?" Jack asked as he entered the morgue.

Lipton turned from the dissection table. "Your body was a male in his twenties. Died, most likely two to three years ago. Last meal appeared to be roast beef and Brussels sprouts. I did a sampling from his hair – no poisons were found, but his hyoid bone was broken. This indicates he was strangled before being placed in the burial space."

"Then why chain him up?" Jack asked.

"Maybe he was chained there – then strangled," Lipton offered.

Jack nodded. "Could have been. Any idea on an ID?"

"I've sent a cast of the deceased's dental profile to the precinct. They'll walk it around to some of the local dentists in the area," Lipton stated.

"Anything else?" Jack asked.

"He had the onset of syphilis," Lipton told Jack.

Taking out the pack of Black Cats, he put one into his mouth. He offered one to Lipton – who took it.

As he lit the man's cigarette, Jack asked, "Have you ever heard of a man called Frauhafer?"

"Doctor Hans Frauhafer, the renowned New York psychiatrist? Yes – most who study medicine have heard of him," Lipton replied. "Has a house along the Palisades and some mansion in Maine I hear and is still the chief of operations at New York City Lunatic Asylum."

Jack smoked as he took out his flask. "A respectable man?"

Lipton leaned back against the steel table. "Don't tell anyone I said this, but I've heard he was involved in some experimental surgeries a few years back that resulted in a few patients being horribly disfigured. He was removed from actively practicing at the hospital, but due to his capital investment in the asylum, they appointed him as chief of operations. Administrative stuff and such."

Jack walked over and handed Lipton the container of liquor. "Anything else I should know?"

"About Frauhafer? He's reputed to be an emotionless man, with a propensity to the occult. Rumors were circulating in 1912 that he was performing inhuman experiments at his home and the asylum.

"Probably not an easy man to see?" Jack asked.

"Probably not," Lipton replied. "Best to call his office – make an appointment."

CHAPTER 5
UNINVITED GUESTS

Jack sat in the foyer to Doctor Frauhafer's office at the Manhattan State Hospital - also known as the old New York City Lunatic Asylum on Ward's Island. The gray ash of his cigarette was nearly halfway to his fingers as he tapped it into the ashtray next to his seat.

A lovely blond woman in a flower print dress approached.

"Agent Parlance?"

Jack stood up. "I am."

"The doctor will see you now. Just through there." She motioned with her hand toward a stout looking and brightly polished ornate wooden door.

Jack nodded. He walked over and entered the office. The large room resembled a small library – two-story bookshelves covered two walls. On the far side was a long wooden desk with all accoutrements. A shaft of bright sunlight flooded in from behind the desk. The window was nearly the height of the wood-paneled wall and framed Frauhafer's workspace. A tall, slender man in a black jacket and dark trousers stood up.

"Agent Parlance from Washington D.C.?" the man asked.

"Doctor Frauhafer?" Jack asked in kind.

"Yes." The doctor motioned for Jack to sit in one of the thick, leather chairs across from his desk. "If you don't mind. I hope this will not take long – I have some business to attend to in twenty minutes." Frauhafer set an odd clock on the center of his desk and pressed down a pin on the top. "This will keep us both honest about the time," he added as he sat down facing Jack. "What can I do for you and those in D.C.?"

Jack took out a cigarette and lit it. "I'm here about the Dobbs disappearance," he said.

"Disappearance? When did this happen?" Frauhafer

seemed surprised and concerned.

"About eleven months ago. I understand that you treated him." Jack spewed out a stream of gray smoke.

"Indeed, I did. His father was very persuasive and concerned about his son's proclivities."

"What sort of treatment did he receive while here?" Jack asked.

"Might I see your credentials first… and is this an official inquiry?" Frauhafer asked.

Jack fished out his badge and handed it to Frauhafer. "It is official. I'm reporting back to D.C. on this case."

Frauhafer nodded, then handed back the badge. "You understand my concern for the privacy of my patients?"

Jack nodded. "The treatment?"

"Standard stuff. Counter conditioning to the offending stimulus, rigid enforcement techniques, and electro-shock to remove the impulse." Frauhafer leaned forward, opened a cigar box, and took one out. He cut off the end, lifted a gold lighter up, and rolled the end of the stogie in the flame as he puffed. "If you like, I can have the treatment files copied for you."

"Please," Jack stated. "Why did Dobbs remove his son from treatment?"

"The father – Henry – was concerned by the burn marks on Jody's temples. He thought that the critical part of the treatment was cruel. In fact – the subject is often unaware of the minor burns as the jolt of electricity affects the memory center of the brain, and the patient rarely is aware of the side effect." Frauhafer drew in a deep volume of smoke, blowing it out up towards the ceiling. "Amazing the power of electricity. All very standard when dealing with those bent on unnatural sexual conduct," he said.

"I understand that Dobbs withdrew a grant to fund some research or building improvements," Jack stated.

"Yes. It was clear we were not on the same – how does one put it – train toward the same station," Frauhafer told Jack. "No matter though – I secured funding through another channel, and the research is moving forward."

"What is the nature of your research? If you don't mind me asking?" Jack tapped his ash into the closest ashtray.

"It has to do with the use of electrical power in the manipulation of brain matter. I'm sure it has no bearing on your investigation Mister Parlance."

"Let me be the judge of that," Jack said.

"Very well." Frauhafer leaned forward and set his cigar in a tray. "We are studying the effects of high voltage high-frequency phase convergence to manipulate the positioning of matter. The measure of this machine will show the change in psychopathy patients' brain structure. I plan on publishing the results next year."

Jack half-smiled. He felt Frauhafer was lying. Something in his manner… his body language… his voice. "Do you know what happened to Jody Dobbs?" Jack's voice was even – void of accusation.

"Neither I nor anyone that I employ here knows what happened to that young man. His base desires were exotic to the point of self-destruction. I would not be surprised if his parents sent him away to protect him. Perhaps exiled to the continent – on the Grand Tour perhaps, or consigned to an abbey in Europe." Frauhafer retrieved his cigar and sat back again.

The chime of a bell rang out into the room. Frauhafer looked at the clock on his desk. "I'm afraid that my time is up, Agent Parlance. I'll walk you out." He stood up and came around the desk.

Jack rose from his chair and followed the doctor toward the door. "So, I have your word that you have not laid eyes on Jody Dobbs since he left your care nearly a year ago?" Jack asked.

Both men walked into the adjacent room.

"You have my word," Frauhafer stated.

Jack stopped at the door leading into the hallway. He shook Frauhafer's hand. "Thank you, Doctor. If I have any further questions, I'll call your assistant. Please have those copies of Dobbs records sent to me at the Lucerne Hotel in Manhattan."

"Good day, Agent Parlance. And I hope that you discover the fate of young Mister Dobbs." Frauhafer turned and headed back toward his office.

Jack left the asylum. He walked several blocks until he came to the busy train station. He waited.

The train went across the bridge carrying visitors and employees of the asylum, residents of the island, and the odd traveler. Next stop – Manhattan.

Jack checked in at his hotel. He sent a telegram to his boss and then headed out to get lunch. Glancing at his wristwatch, he noted the time – 1:30 p.m.

He stopped at a Jewish deli and ate. Once done, he headed back to the hospital to talk to Doctor Lipton.

"I want you to know that I've done something unusual, Agent Parlance," Lipton said as Jack came into the room.

"What is that?" Jack asked.

"I went and took a look at the murder scene. There were things missed earlier. Here they are." Lipton pulled away a white cloth to expose remnants of rope and a couple of pulleys.

"What am I looking at?" Jack asked.

"I have a hypothesis," Lipton began. "I think our victim was walled up alive. This," he held up some fragments of rope, "was looped around his neck and set with a gallows knot. It could be tightened but can't be easily loosened. The pulleys were used to provide the victim his own choice of death. Probably looped around his foot to allow him the ability to step down to pull the rope tight. The person, or persons who did this to him, are a fiendish sort. Imagine you are walled up. No water, no food. Spiders and rats are about – maybe even already looking at you as a meal. You can wait and hope you die of thirst before anything is gnawed off – or you can manipulate the rope to strangle yourself – putting an end to your torment."

Jack pulled out a cigarette and offered one to Lipton. "So, it was torture?"

"Exactly – and of the sort that the imposer is satisfied not to have to witness. A psychopath perhaps. Someone deliberate – well planned – and not to be underestimated," Lipton said as he lit his smoke. "If I were you, keep your pistol handy, and if you run across that sort – kill before he has the chance to kill you."

"Thanks, Doc," Jack said as he handed Lipton a piece of paper. This is where I'm staying while in Manhattan. If you have any other insights, call me here." Jack turned and headed out.

Jody was at that house. Did he have a hand at murdering the other fellow? Jack hailed a cab.

As he headed back to his hotel, he noticed that the odd car with mirror-windows followed him – a few cars back. They seemed to know how to put on a tail. He looked forward and thought on Dobbs.

Stubbing out his cigarette in the small ashtray, he said, "Hey, Mac, pull over up here." Jack fished out a couple of bucks.

The cab stopped, and Jack handed the driver the cash. "Keep it," he said as he got out. The car pulled away and he turned, looking into one of the expansive plate-glass windows that lined the sidewalk.

The black Hudson was parked across the street. Jack watched it from the reflection. The doors did not open, nor did the car move as he stood there.

"Alright," he whispered. "You want to play? Let's play."

He turned away from the direction of the car and began walking. After a few minutes, he came to Parky's Italiano Restaurante. Jack went inside.

Across the room was a set of booths – not well lit, a burning candle mounted on a sangria bottle, a checkered red and white tablecloth hanging down. He didn't wait to be seated – instead, just went and sat.

A young dark-haired man came quickly and smiled at Jack. "Can I get you a menu?" His Italian accent was heavy.

"Ya. And you got a crapper in this joint?" Jack asked.

The man looked surprised. "Of course. Go down that hall, and out back. The toilet is through the blue painted door. You can't miss it."

Jack nodded and stood. He glanced out the window. By the corner was a tall fellow in an overcoat and white straw hat looking in.

Moving down the hallway, Jack stopped near the kitchen entrance and waited – watching to see if the man entered the establishment

A moment passed, and the man came in. His face was expressionless – dull, pale, drawn like that of a corpse.

In a muffled voice, Jack heard – "The man who came in here. Where did he go?"

The Italian waiter looked nervous. "What is this about?"

"I'm asking the questions!" the stranger said in a monotone as he held out what looked to be a shield-wallet. "Where is he?"

"He went to use the john – out back," the young waiter stated.

Jack slipped outside and moved to the restroom. He went inside, then opened the door and stepped out, making for the restaurant again. Inside the doorway, he saw a shadowy figure quickly retreat.

Returning to his booth, Jack sat down. This time, the strange man was sitting near the large window. The young Italian brought the man a cup of what appeared to be espresso.

Jack waited, then ordered. The young man brought out a helping of lasagna, a glass of root beer, and some bread.

Who was that guy? Another bureau agent? Secret Service? Treasury? A mobster? Jack was keeping an eye on the fellow. The guy was lanky but big. Jack hoped he'd not need to put the arm on him anytime soon. But, if he did, the knuckle-dusters in his pocket and the sap in his coat would help balance things out.

Pushing his plate away, he finished his root beer and ate the remaining buttered bread. Dabbing his mouth with the napkin, he tossed four bits on the table, then made for the door.

The street was busy – cabs, personal vehicles, and a streetcar. People were coming and going chaotically – crisscrossing the road, avoiding being killed by automobiles.

Taking out his pack of Black Cats, he flipped one into his mouth, brought up his lighter, shielded the flame with his cupped hands. From the corner of his eye, he saw the tail – the man standing at the intersection of an ally across the street – watching him.

Jack stopped at the corner, hailed a cab. Getting in, he said, "201 West 79th Street. The Lucerne Hotel."

"Got it, bub!" the cabbie said, his Brooklyn accent heavy.

The black and white checkered cab sped away from the curb. Jack glanced back over his shoulder - the Hudson was not far behind.

CHAPTER 6
TEMPLE OF DESPAIR

As Jack entered the hotel, he went straight to the courtesy phone. "Give me an outside line," he said. "Operator? Connect me to the 19th police station. "Yes – precinct – thank you." Jack was quiet as the operator did her thing. Hello – this is Agent Jack Parlance for Detective Hurston. I'll wait."

A few moments passed as Jack fished out another cigarette and lit it off the one in his mouth.

"Detective Hurston? The connection is a bit poor. I can hear you. Do you have a tail on me?" Jack drew in the acrid smoke and let it leak out the side of his mouth. "Any reason another detective would?" he watched the front entrance. No, a tall man in an overcoat and straw hat came in. "Ya – someone's taken an interest in me. They're competent. I think they want me to know they're following me. I make two – one in a dark Hudson with mirrored windows, and another that can get out and follow on foot. Yes – I said mirrored windows – like mirrors, not regular glass." Okay – I appreciate it." Jack chuckled. "I know I'm pushing that professional courtesy thing."

Hanging up the phone, Jack went to the front desk. "Any messages?"

The middle-aged man regarded Jack's key, then looked behind the desk. "Here you go, sir." He handed Jack a sealed Western Union envelope.

Once up in his room, Jack opened the telegram and read it.

AA09
MGA646 DL= NY MI ITN⁻
MR PARLANCE=
LUCERNE HOTLE 201 WEST 79TH STREET MANHATTAN NY=

LOOK IN BASEMENT OF ASCH BUILDING. HIDDEN ROOM. =

MMPP INVOLVED. REACHES HIGHEST LEVELS.

1000 AM 12 B BTKY 73 QFA BN.

Outside the window, the sky was growing dark. Jack put the note into his satchel, then left to go find dinner. He was feeling strangely tired. A sense of weariness was settling in, and he craved a good sleep.

Back in the lobby, he asked at the reception desk. "Do you know where I can find the Asch building?"

The man narrowed his eyes. "Why?"

"Do I need a reason?" Jack asked, annoyed.

"You don't know what that place is?"

Jack grew impatient. "Evidently, not if it's such a secret."

The man looked upon Jack as if he were from Mars. "It's just the opposite, sir. I thought everyone knew of the Triangle Shirttail Factory fire."

Jack was taken back. "That's where the fire happened?"

"It was. If you don't mind, why would you ask if you didn't know its gruesome past?" the clerk inquired

A moment passed. "That's an excellent question," Jack replied, turned on his heels and made for the door.

The meatloaf was greasier than Jack cared for, but the mashed potatoes and green peas were prepared just right.

He pushed away the plate and sat back to enjoy a smoke. Outside of the diner, the ever-evolving darkness of Manhattan aged gracefully. Few pedestrians were out. Few automobiles lumbered up and down the paved street.

He paid twenty-five cents for the food and left a nickel tip for the glass of wine the owner served him. The proprietor provided wine to any patron who showed an interest in his private vintage – and all did.

Jack walked the two blocks back to the hotel – ever vigilant for the errant Hudson lurking about. As he passed the alleys, he noted well-dressed people coming and going from one of the side doors – Jazz blaring from the portal as it opened and closed. Just another example of the failure to legislate morality. Did Jody Dobbs travel with such a crowd?

As he entered the hotel, Jack checked his watch – 10:30 p.m. He stopped in the middle of the lobby to light his Black Cat. Looking up, he saw Lipton standing there.

"Doctor Lipton," Jack said. "Something I can do for you?"

Lipton looked concerned. "Agent Parlance. Something's come up. The body of the dead man and all the evidence has gone missing." Lipton took out a pack of Old Gold cigarettes and drew one out with his lips. He stopped and offered one to Jack, who indicated with his current half-smoked cigarette that he had one already. "Yes… yes, of course, you have one…"

"What happened?" Jack demanded.

"Some men paid me a visit. Something terribly off with them," Lipton said.

"White straw hats? Dull eyes – expressionless faces?"

Lipton looked surprised. With a shaking hand, he brought his smoke up to his lips. "Yes."

"They've been following me around lately. Any idea who they are?" Jack asked.

"They showed me a badge – but I didn't recognize the branch of law enforcement. Something to do with the War Department, I think."

"So, what has you so shaken?" Jack inquired.

"They're very presence," Lipton stated. "And… I can't account for a few hours. They came to see me in the morgue. We talked. I answered their questions. Then, two hours of my day are gone. The next thing I remember is standing over a stiff with a scalpel in my hand. I can't remember anything about the previous couple of hours."

"Some kind of gas, or maybe you were injected with something?" Jack was concerned.

"Nothing apparent – and if only I could remember something…" Lipton began to tremble and sat down.

"Steady old-man," Jack said. Sitting down, he fished out his flask and handed it to the doctor.

Lipton took a long drag from his smoke. "Somewhere in the back of my mind, I feel like I saw something. Something I wasn't supposed to see… or aren't able to fully comprehend."

"I can understand," Jack stated. "During the war, I saw something I've never been able to make sense of. There were lots of terrible things – but this thing I saw was…" Jack too put his cigarette between his lips and drew in. "To this day, I'm not sure if I was rattled by the artillery fire and hallucinated it, or if it was real. It couldn't be real," Jack whispered.

Lipton appeared to rally. The color came back to his face, and the man got to his feet. "I'm going to go home now and lock myself in. I sure as hell don't want to meet those guys again. Hey – thanks for the snort!"

Jack nodded and took back the flask. He, too, stood, then watched as Lipton exited through the front. Turning, Jack went back to his room.

As he came along the hallway, he saw that his door was ajar. Removing his pistol, he crept toward the portal. The light was on. Putting his left hand on the door, he opened it slowly. The room was a wreck. And, standing there was Detective Hurston and two policemen.

CHAPTER 7
A HOLE IN ONE

"Howdy, Jack," Hurston stated. "Come on in."

Jack entered and put his pistol back into its holster. "What's the rumpus?"

Hurston put his pipe into his mouth and lit a match. "We got a call that there was a disturbance in this room. I'd flagged your name, so when the duty officer heard you were the occupant, I got the alert. When we arrived, the door was open, and the place was like this."

Jack went over to the small bureau. The drawers were pulled out and were scattered across the floor. He pulled the chest away from the wall and retrieved his satchel from behind it.

"Neat trick," Hurston said.

"Ya – these hotel dressers were built with an extension along the wall. Just big enough to put a valuable behind." Jack thumbed through his documents. "All here."

"Any ideas who might have tossed your room?" Hurston took a puff from his pipe.

"Probably the same yeggs who've been tailing me," Jack postulated.

"I had a couple of men watch your hotel to see if that car came by. If that Hudson was involved, they must have parked somewhere else and walked in."

Jack chuckled. "The end to a perfect night. How'd they break in?"

"Not sure, but probably picked the door lock," Hurston stated. "I'll let you know if we find anything to tell us who did this."

Jack nodded. "Well – I guess I need a new room." He left and caught the elevator. Once he secured another room, he asked the desk clerk, "Did a man wearing a white straw hat ask about me?"

"As a matter of fact, two men came in and asked about you. They said they wanted to leave you a note on your door."

"And you obliged them?" Jack was perturbed.

"Of course. They showed me their badges," the clerk said.

Jack's jaw tightened. "Pass the word – if anyone asks about me in the future – have them leave a message here, and no one is to tell them what room I'm in. Got it?"

The clerk was visibly intimidated. "Yes, sir. My apologies, sir. But they had badges…"

"That don't mean shit, sonny," Jack replied. "Make sure you pass my instructions along."

"I will," the clerk replied – conviction in his voice.

Jack took a room at the far end of the fifth floor. This time, he was going to be a little smarter when it came to personal security.

* * *

Jack got out of the taxi. As he moved toward the Asch building, he noted two tall men dressed in dark black suits wearing white straw hats approach.

"Agent Parlance?" one asked, his voice disturbingly monotone. He showed an identification document on glossy paper then a badge.

"You are interfering in a highly sensitive national security matter. Those who are at the very top have directed us to tell you to cease your investigation into the Dobbs boy, or you will be de-ceased. We have no patients for your meddling."

The man's features never changed – he was for all intents and purposes – expressionless.

"Who the God damn hell do you think you are?" Jack challenged. "I ought to bust you in the mouth for threatening me, you son-of-a-bitch!"

The other one came close. "That would be unwise." His voice was the same as the other – indistinguishable. "I'd hate to see your house burned down – and Mister Pinkerton suffer the agony of burning to death."

Jack's meaty fist flew and smashed into the first fellow's jaw. The man rocked back but did not go down. His chin was crooked, and the skin around his face distorted. The stranger, with his hands, readjusted his face back into order. He remained expressionless.

"We will give you until tomorrow to see reason. Then we will have to report up our chain. Keep seeking – and you will reap an unpleasant outcome."

The two men turned in unison and walked away, crossing the street. They got into the dark Hudson with mirrored windows. The vehicle raced off silently down the road, abruptly turned a corner, and was gone.

Jack un-clinched his fists. His blood was up, and he desperately wanted to fight more. Taking out his small notebook, he scrawled down – Contact made with odd men dressed in black suits, wearing straw hats and makeup. They carry credentials – but unknown department. Large men – 6', 4" or so, brown eyes, short dark hair, broad jaw, wide face. Can take a solid punch and bounce back. Next time – use knuckle-dusters and sap – hope it doesn't come to shooting.

He put back the small pad into his vest pocket, then continued across the street to the Asch building. Ten stories of steel framework and stone façade climbed into the sky. It was by no means the tallest building now in New York, but it was significant. The Asch building had the dubious honor of being the site of the most heinous negligence against workers yet known – the massive fire killing hundreds of women working for the Triangle Shirtwaist Factory.

Jack stopped on the street – he thought on the broken bones and burnt flesh of those poor women who threw themselves from the upper floors to escape the sweeping blaze. He looked up – eighty feet – one hell of a long way to fall, Jack thought.

The building had streams of people coming and going through the double lobby doors. Students carrying bundles of books passed Jack as he entered.

He passed through the crowd and headed down a hallway. At the end, he found the building manager's office and knocked.

"Come in!" came the reply.

Jack entered. "Good day. I'm Agent Jack Parlance from the Bureau of Investigation - Washington D.C. I'm investigating the disappearance of a young man."

"I'm Dale Parker, the building manager. How can I help you, Detective Parlance?" The red-haired man stood and reached his hand across the narrow desk.

Jack shook the man's hand. "I need access to your subfloor – the basement. Would you mind giving me access?"

Dale smiled. "Sure. Mind if I see some credentials, though?"

Jack produced his badge. Dale grabbed a ring of keys. "Well, follow me."

They went down a set of switchback stairs, descending into a dimly-lit brick hallway painted white. At the end, Dale opened a door with a key, and they both went in.

"This is a strange place at times," Dale said over his shoulder.

"How so?" Jack asked.

"Maintenance workers and some of the tenants up on the top floors have reported seeing and hearing strange things."

"Like?" Jack pursued.

"I had one lady tell me she heard whispers late at night. One man told me, as he was leaving his office, he heard screams coming from floor eight. One of my men, while fixing a pipe down here, saw a woman walk through a wall."

"So, ghosts…" Jack said. He didn't hide his skepticism.

"Damn right, ghosts!" Dale replied. "I've even seen a few myself." Dale stopped. "So, why is it you want to go down here, and what are you looking for?"

Jack took out a Black Cat.

"No! I'm sorry, but you can't smoke down here. Sometimes – and it is rare – gas can leak in these old buildings and... well I'm sure I don't have to explain what can happen when gas meets a flame," Dale stated.

Jack nodded and put the pack away. "I'm looking for a hidden room, or maybe a small room seldom used."

"There is a strange room we call the Olsen Room. It is original to the building, and we've only speculated as to what it was for."

"Take me there," Jack directed.

"Okay, it's this way," Dale said.

"So, what have you come up with?" Jack asked.

"Well, we think they're symbols related to Masons. The original builders – I mean, the architects – probably belonged to the Masons who may have done a prebuild ritual in it." Dale stopped and produced a flashlight. He turned it on and crouched down as he pulled open a vault-like door.

"We won't get locked in here, will we?" Jack had some concerns.

"No – there's no locking mechanic. The door is original but seems to only hide the access and not prevent access – if you know what I mean," Dale replied.

There was a sudden chill. The air in the space was so cold Jack could see his breath puffing out.

"Here we are," Dale said.

An octagonal room twenty feet across erupted from the end of the tunnel. Jack and Dale stood up.

"Look at the walls," Dale said as he shined his light.

There were impressions made into each cement wall. Jack went and examined one. The figure of a man with a crocodile head was holding a jar of something. Dale moved the light to the next figure. A dog-headed man, then a bird-headed man. The images had different animal heads, but all were attached to the body of a man.

"See – strange stuff. Look at the floor." Dale focused

the beam of light on the middle of the floor. A square and compass were pressed into the floor and filled in with some sort of material that began glowing and shifting like a metallic fluid. It shimmered in the light.

"Now – watch this," Dale said and turned out the light.

The room fell into darkness, but a dark blue glow began to fill the space from the center.

Dale pointed upward.

"Look at that," Jack said.

The ceiling was filled with tiny white, blue, and red lights.

"I've been in this room a dozen times, and it never gets old!" Dale said – excitement filling his voice.

"Close this tunnel and room off. No one is to enter. Some police officers will be by. They will interview anyone who has been in this room – so make me a list of all those you or your people can think of who have been in here," Jack told Dale.

Jack and Dale left and moved back to the lobby of the building. Jack provided the manager with his hotel name.

"Call me at the Lucerne Hotel. They'll get the message to me. Don't discuss this with anyone other than the local police and me. No one else, no matter what credentials they show you. Refer anyone else to me." Jack looked over his shoulder.

"Sure," Dale stated. "What's this all about again?"

"I'll be back later today with a cameraman. Be available," Jack said. He turned and left the building.

He hailed a black and white checkered cab and headed to the 19th Precinct.

CHAPTER 8
SHADOWS OF COURSE

The train car jiggled left then right as the clack of the wheels drummed out a dull drone. He took from his satchel the teletype document from his boss about John Woolley. The man had been the original architect, and Jack was on his way to see him at his house near Nyack Beach on the Hudson.

He put the document back and took out the picture of the little room's ceiling. Jack viewed the images of the small chamber below the Asch building. They reminded him of the Howard Carter pictures. In the middle of the room, inscribed around the Mason symbols were the Latin phrases - Acta deos numquam mortalia fallunt, and Vincit qui se vincit.

Turning one of the pictures over in his hand, Jack evaluated the pattern of fuzzy white specks the cameraman had captured covering the roof. It appeared to be a star constellation, but Jack wasn't sure. So, he'd sent a copy of the picture to an astronomer at New York University.

The train was slowing and coming into the station. The carriages were clanking as the breaks were applied, and the long chain of cars rattled to a halt.

Jack found a cab and had the driver deliver him to Wooley's home. The car dropped him off at a wrought iron gate flanked by two ten-foot-high gray stone gateposts. He looked along the road at the twelve-foot-high stone wall that ran the highway's length in both directions. The only view was through the black metal bars at an elaborate five-story Georgian style manor house.

Lifting the latch on the gate, Jack entered and walked along the gravel lane toward the massive home and the separate adjacent two-story auto-garage.

A twelve-foot-high white double door served as the main entrance, and Jack rapped his fist against it. A moment later, a butler appeared.

"Yes?"

"I'm Agent Parlance with the Washington D.C. Bureau of Investigation. I'd like to speak to Mister Wooley."

The servant appeared annoyed. "Did you make an appointment?"

"No. I'm investigating a missing person," Jack said.

"Ah – in that case… Make an appointment and come back when you have a confirmation that you are invited – Agent Parlance." The butler began to close the door.

Jack blocked the door with his foot. "I hear what you're saying," Jack said. "But, I've come along way, and if you don't go and tell Mister Wooley that I'm here to see him, I'm going drag you out here and beat you within an inch of your life – bub. Now, turn yourself around, find your boss, and I'll wait in here." Jack pushed his way into the foyer.

The fancy-dressed man stared at Jack – who in a moment of transparency flashed the man his badge. The butler gave a heavy sigh, turned, and vanished through the cavernous space, past the two opposing curved stairwells, and down a dark hallway.

Jack stood by a large round table in the middle of the entryway. A white porcelain vase filled with fresh tulips sat in the center of the marble surface.

Jack looked around. Eight yellow marble columns held up the two-story roof. The detailed crown molding – the stamped copper accents – gave the roof an expensive appearance.

"The wooden molding is from a sixteenth-century castle in Scotland," a voice said behind Jack. "The stamped patterns are duplicates of what a master craftsman made in plaster for a home in Devonshire – late 1740s if I remember correctly."

Turning, Jack saw an older man approaching. His clean, shaved face beamed with a toothy smile.

"Are you interested in ancient architecture, Agent Parlance?"

Jack smiled and extended his hand. "Mister Wooley, I presume?"

"No presumption about it – I am John Wooley." The man shook Jack's hand.

John was a little taller than half of Jack's height, slightly stooped – walking with a polished wooden cane topped with a silver handle.

"Shall we move to a more comfortable room? Andre – please bring us some coffee in the Osiris Room." Wooley shouted.

Jack followed the man to a set of tall beige doors. Wooley pushed them open and entered a splendid parlor covered in golden wallpaper. The ceiling was like the entryway – ornate with crafted wood accents. The far end had floor-to-ceiling windows that let in the bright sunlight and overlooked an ever-expanding yard of dark green grass.

Wooley sat on one of two couches that faced each other – separated by a long cocktail table.

Jack sat opposite his host. The man set his cane against the side of the couch and crossed his left leg over his right and leaned back.

"My man tells me you are investigating a missing person. How can I help?" Wooley asked.

"As part of my investigation, I discovered the small ritualistic room in the basement of the Asch building you designed," Jack began.

Wooley blurted a laugh, then nodded. "The room… Yes, sort of a joke as I remember."

"A joke?" Jack asked.

"You see, I belong to a certain group. I'm not allowed to say, but I believe you can guess. I was directed to build the room for a ritual that we performed before setting the building's first cornerstone. Some might call it superstition, but in some ways, it is a charming ancient practice that makes lofty men feel like they have more control over their lives than they do." Wooley clasped his fingers and hooked them over his knee.

"Coffee is served," announced Andre as he came into the room with a maid carrying a silver tray topped with cups and a carafe.

The maid laid out the cups and saucers, then poured the dark-black coffee. The smell of the freshly brewed grounds was intoxicating. The servants left.

"The person in whom you are interested?" Wooley asked.

Jack took up his cup and blew across the surface to cool it. Steam rushed away with each puff.

"Are you familiar with the Dobbs family?" Jack inquired.

"Of course. Few who live in this great state don't. I was even considered as one of the architects for a project Henry Dobbs was managing for the Vanderbilt's – the Marble House." Wooley sat forward and took a sip.

"Have you ever met Henry Dobbs's son, Jody?" Jack pressed.

"Not ever," Wooley stated.

"Back to the purpose of the room. What exactly was the ritual?"

Wooley sat silent for a moment, then chuckled. "I guess there's no harm in telling. It is mostly nonsense, really. The Freemasons go back thousands of years – to the earliest days when men turned from living as wild animals and began shaping stone to form foundations of civilization. As such, the ritual conducted in that particular basement – was intended to connect the spirit of the building with the spirit of the immortal. A… sort of… celestial insurance to keep the building from falling– affected by acts of God and such."

"Didn't help when it came to the fire," Jack said.

"I said acts of God… or maybe even gods. Not the acts of men." Wooly sipped his coffee.

"The iconography on the walls of that room?" Jack took out a Black Cat and put it into his mouth.

"Egyptian immortals – each an embodiment of the elements of nature and the heavens."

"And the ceiling – a star constellation?" Jack furthered.

Wooley smiled. "Very good, Agent Parlance. It is indeed. Orion's Belt to be exact… and the stars around it."

"Why? What does it mean?"

"We architects are a funny lot. We mix the aesthetic with the emotional. Mood, light, passion, love, hate, longing – we want those who enter the space we build to feel these things. Have a very individual and personal experience. Do you like art, Agent Parlance?" Wooley asked.

"Some – typically, I don't know what to like about it."

"You're not alone. Most people don't know how to view artworks. Fewer know about the world and the universe at large. But most do know when they've been touched by some stimulus that peeks their emotions." Wooley uncrossed his legs, re-crossing them the opposite way. He drank down more of his coffee. "Would you be interested in staying for lunch?"

Jack was taken off guard. Wooley smiled at him.

"Thank you, but no. I'm expected back in Manhattan soon." Jack finished his coffee and set the cup down on the saucer.

Wooley sat forward. "The images in the room – did they stimulate you at all?"

"What?" Jack asked, surprised at the question.

"Emotions – seeing the reliefs? What did you feel when you first saw them?" Wooley asked.

"Surprised, scared. For a moment. I felt as if I was trapped in that room. What was I supposed to feel?"

Wooley chuckled again. "I intended that the room give one the feeling of traveling through space – passing from one world to another – stimulating the feeling of fear – longing – discovery – passion. But my audience was other Freemasons, not the general public. No one was intended to see it again. I'm glad that you liked the freezes, though."

He took another drink. "Horton Pilipy was the artist who created them. All I did was design the space."

"So, the artwork was done by someone else?"

"Typical," Wooley stated. "All the architect does is design – others do the building and artwork. At least most of the time."

"Do you have his address?"

"As I remember, a small town in Upstate. Something Irish… yes, Ulster, I think," Wooly stated. "I'll have Andre provide it to you before you leave." Wooley reached over to the side-table and pressed a button. A moment later, Andre appeared.

"Sir?"

"Please go to my study and provide Agent Parlance with the address of Horton Pilipy."

"Yes, sir. Right away, sir. Shall I have the maid come clear away your coffee?"

Wooley sat forward and poured more of the black-coffee into both his and Jack's cups. "Soon, Andre – soon."

Wooley had his chauffeur drive Jack to the train station. From there, Jack took the 2:15 p.m. train back to Manhattan.

Once back at his hotel, he drafted several detailed reports and had the information sent via teletype to the bureau. Then, he sent a Western Union telegram to Ms. Hastings, asking her to take Mr. Pinkerton into protective custody until he returned. The warning of the two mysterious men was weighing on his mind.

Jack asked the man working behind the desk for a referral card for the Mouse Tale gin-joint that McFadden owned just down the street. The young man looked concerned.

"Don't worry, fella. I'm just interested in a drink. I'm not going to blow the whistle." Taking out his flask, Jack offered the lad some.

The attendant smiled and took a slug. He handed back the container and went into the back office. Returning, he handed Jack a special certificate – a card that allowed those not known to the establishment to get access.

"Also allows you into the casino," the young man said.

Jack nodded. Thanks, bub. Don't worry, I ain't looking to make any trouble." He made sure there were no messages, then went out for dinner. After, he would stop at McFadden's speakeasy.

Jack waited near the door of the speakeasy. A drunken couple – the woman dressed in a dark mink, and the man in a black and white tuxedo staggered up. A few people queued up behind them.

Taking in the intense tobacco smoke from one of his Black Cats, Jack waited.

The man rapped on the door. Jack heard a mumble. Though the man was quiet, Jack made out the words. The door came open, and the couple went in.

Casually glancing over, Jack noted the door was still open, and the gorilla in the doorway was getting the password from each as he allowed entry. Jack got in line. Others lined up behind him.

He got to the door. Jack took out a fiver and palmed it. The bouncer looked him up and down with dull eyes.

"Ya?" The bruiser of a man asked.

Jack handed the man the card. "Jumping Jack sent me."

The tough looked at the card, took the money, then nodded and let Jack in.

Jazz music was blasting from the stage. The band leader was bobbing and twitching – really putting on the heat – a real hep cat.

CHAPTER 9
GIN JOINT JIVE

The joint was jumping. Jack was directed to a table and brought some shelled peanuts – heavily salted. He took a handful and munched until the waitress came by to take his drink order.

"Scotch – and not the paint – I'll know the difference," Jack told her.

The girl was momentarily disoriented. "Uh… okay. You know something I don't?" She seemed sincerely interested.

"What'd ya think?" Jack took out a smoke and lit it. "Send the gasper-girl around. I'm running low on smokes."

The waitress hustled off. A moment later, a blond bearcat of a woman came over. She oozed attitude and gave Jack a look up and down. "What'll it be, bub?"

Jack almost cracked a smile. "Butt me with a pack." He put a dollar on her tray. She eyed it hungrily. "Keep it. I'll take the Black Cats."

She pulled up a pack and handed it to Jack.

The waitress came by and put a glass of scotch on the table. She looked at the cigarette girl, and they nodded – it was subtle.

He sipped his drink and watched the madcap chaos as men and women danced, patrons came and went in herds, and jazz music raged over the din.

"You here for fun or business?" The voice was behind Jack, a few feet away – maybe.

Slowly Jack turned in his seat. Sitting in a chair – a light blue suit, diamond stickpin, gold rings on most of his fingers. The man's face was jovial – a mirthful smile, crinkled lines at the outer corners of his eyes.

"So, you ain't no yegg," the man said. He leaned in and sniffed the air. "Aqua Velva." He sat back again. "You're a dick," he said as he shook his head. "A bent dick at that –

or are you planning to roll the joint?"

Jack didn't smile. He recognized the man – Jimmy McKerry.

"Was on the prowl, feeling a bit daffy and thought I'd drop in on Ms. McFadden and my soon to be best pal Jimmy McKerry," Jack said.

Jimmy's expression of jocularity vanished. "Who the hell are you, pal?

Jack reached up and took the cigarette from his mouth and exhaled out the corner of this mouth into the thick smokey haze of the gin joint. "Don't get excited. No one's in for the pinch. I'm here for a drink and some polite palaver."

Jimmy slowly stood.

"Easy cake-eater – I'm – I'm not muscling in on nothing. I got a job to do, and you and your lady-boss are part of it. Be a good fellow and let Ms. McFadden know Agent Jack Parlance wishes to have a chat."

Jimmy cracked a smile. He liked being called a cake-eater. "Now? Here?"

"Here, there – wherever," Jack said. "But I'm only here a few days, and I need the info. I'll throw in some berries for your trouble – a few sawbucks, or even a couple of bones if you're friendly enough."

Jimmy appeared to be sizing Jack up. "Stay here, I'll be back." He vanished into the crowd toward the back of the building.

Jack shot back his scotch and ordered another. He sat watching the show – eyeing the crowd and thinking.

Checking his watch, Jack noted it was 2:21 a.m. He was about to leave when a blond-haired doll with gams that could change a man's religion approached. Her sparkling white sequence dress radiated light from every direction.

Jack looked on enthralled as she glided with the gracefulness of a ship sliding into its berth. She stopped in front of him. Behind her was Jimmy.

"I hear you want to talk to me. You don't look like the average flat-foot." Her sultry voice could have melted a steel girder.

She pulled up a chair and sat with her knees slightly apart. She lifted her hand, and a waitress came over, set down another scotch on Jack's table, then departed. Jimmy sat to the side.

Jack cleared his throat. "I'm a Bureau of Investigation agent from D.C." He took out his badge, held it in his lap, and exposed it to her.

"Bureau of Investigation? Never heard of it," Brenda said.

"It's legit, Ms. McFadden," Jack replied.

"You can call me Brenda." She extended her dainty hand. Jack shook it softly. "What can my associate here or I do for you, agent?"

"Parlance – Jack Parlance." He looked into her dazzling, emerald-colored eyes. "I'm trying to trace the movements of a man who's gone missing. A dandy named Jody Dobbs. Did you know him?"

She cracked a smile. "He was a regular. But the humdrum of my joint wasn't to his taste. He liked… shall we say the forbidden fruits of our city."

"He's vanished. If you've heard of anything that could help me find him, I'll make it work your while," Jack said.

Brenda looked over at Jimmy, then back. "If he's gone, we had nothing to do with it. He kept a strange gaggle of oddballs in his company. He talked a lot about an island off the coast of Florida. Tried to talk me into sailing with his twisted sort there. God knows what hedonistic things would have been done to me." She smiled wickedly at Jack. "If he's anywhere, he's probably there."

"Anything else?" Jack asked.

"There was this place outside the city – a ways up-state. Small town called…" Brenda gazed off into the darkness of the room. "Ulster Park. Yes – that was the name. I remember because he made it a point to say 'Like the county in Ireland' every time he said it."

"Ulster Park? Anything noteworthy about that place?" Jack removed one of his cards and wrote on it, then handed it to Brenda.

Brenda looked at the card. "No, but I suspected it was a den of inequity – a real Sodom and Gamora kinda place."

Jack looked thoughtful. "He made that sort of impression?"

She chuckled. "The things he whispered into my ear... I almost had Jimmy here throw him and his friends out. But – they were laying out a lot of cash in those days."

Jack nodded. "Contact me at my hotel if you remember anything else. I wrote the address on the card." He looked around, downed his drink in one draft, then stood up. "I like your place," he stated as he put down a fifty-dollar bill on the table. "Courtesy of your Uncle Sam," Jack said. He stubbed out his cigarette in the ashtray and headed for the door.

The walk to his hotel was short. He was keenly aware of a tail – but this time, he knew who it was – Jimmy McKerry. Jack made for his room right off. He had little energy to confront the curious McKerry in the lobby.

Once in his room, he felt the force of the whiskey kicking in. He kicked off his shoes and laid down. The liquor was causing him to have odd dreams as he tossed and turned. Faces shouted at him – his lost friends - those men from the war – they never let him rest for long.

Bang – the door vibrated hard, and Jack bolted upright. He reached for his 45 and got to his feet. The door rattled again as someone hit it with considerable force.

"Who is it?" Jack demanded.

A childish giggle was the answer.

Jack slid the bolt to the side and opened the door. There was no one there. He stepped into the hallway. The warm glow of the low incandescent lights made the passageway appear unearthly.

Another giggle drew Jack's attention. At the end of the hall, by the elevator doors, a child stood. In his hand was a large round sucker on a stick. The kid was dressed in a blue and white sailor suit, nickers, black buckled shoes, and wearing a sizeable round-brim hat with a yellow ribbon hanging down on the side.

"Where's your mommy?" Jack called.

The child looked at Jack with a gentle and heart-warming smile. "Dead – like all of us," he said in an impish voice, then walked through the closed lift doors.

The hallway was empty. The elevator dinged, and the doors opened. The operator was standing there looking at Jack.

"Sir? Did you want to use the lift?"

Jack approached. "I didn't ring for it." He looked back down the hall toward his room, then back at the young man in the lift. "There was a child…"

The young man chuckled. "That's Otis," he said. "A small boy in an old-timey outfit – short-pants and funny hat?"

"Yes."

"Yup – that was Otis, alright."

"Who the hell is Otis?" Jack demanded.

"The boy who fell down the elevator shaft some twenty years ago. His mother died shortly after when she hung herself in her room on this very floor."

The buzzer went off inside the elevator.

"I'm needed on floor three. Have a good morning, sir." He closed the doors, and the elevator needle showed the car descending.

"God damned ghosts!" Jack said under his breath – he then became aware he was still holding his service pistol. He tucked it into his belt and headed back to his room.

Looking at his wristwatch, Jack noted the time – 5:50 a.m. He shaved, did a whore's bath, put on clean underclothes, slacks, tweed jacket, accouterments, and splashed some Aqua Velva on his face. Stopping just outside the door, he took a long look down the hallway to the elevator. Did he dream the little boy? Did it happen? Now he was not sure. The lift operator was real... or was he. Jack grunted and headed for the stairs.

Once downstairs, he checked for messages, then went out, caught a cab to the train station.

Boarding the train to Ulster Park, he sat back and reviewed his notes on the case. He had no information on Horton Pilipy. The teletype office at the train station sent his query to the head office in D.C. It would take some time to get a response – if he got a reply at all. The address was old – fifteen years out of date. Pilipy might have moved or died. Jack hoped he had done neither.

By 9:30 a.m., the northbound train stopped at the Ulster station. It was the typical small-town affair – five buildings set up adjacent to the tracks. A raised platform allowed the traveler to easily step off the train onto level ground.

Only a handful of people got off. Jack followed a few of them to the street in front of the station's main office. A black Model T was there – on top, a black sign with white letters read 'Taxi'.

Jack gave the man the address and sat back with a cigarette in his mouth.

"That's few miles outside town," the driver stated.

"Is that a problem?" Jack asked.

"No, sir. I just don't often get folks wanting to head out into that part of the county."

The fellow started the car, and off they went through the small sleepy town of Ulster Park.

They went down the main street. Quaint shops lined the path – general store, pharmacy, hotel, public house. Toward the end, brick homes gave way to stone and wood colonial houses. White picket fences encircled many of them, and more than a couple had well-groomed yards containing flower beds and old trees.

A few times, they passed a Ford truck – a farmer's flatbed stacked with chickens, or produce, headed to town.

"What brings ya to Ulster Park?" the cabbie asked.

"I'm looking for someone," Jack replied.

"I know most in these parts. Who you want?"

"I'm here to visit Horton Pilipy," Jack said.

"Then you should have come here a couple of weeks ago. Old man Pilipy died last Saturday," the cabbie told Jack. "If you're heading to his place – he ain't home no more."

"Died? What happened," Jack asked.

The cabbie glanced over his shoulder. "Poor old fool done tripped and fell down his stairs. Snapped his neck like breaking a carrot in half. A friend of his… a neighbor, found him the following day. They said he was lying there twisted up, his eyes fixed on the top of the stairs from where he fell. Chills me just thinking about it."

"What's the name of the person who found him?" Jack furthered.

"Harry York. His home is just a mile up the road from Mr. Pilipy's place. Do you want me to turn around and take you back to town?"

Jack took a long drag from his Black Cat, then blew the smoke out the window. "No, take me to Pilipy's home.

CHAPTER 10
DISTURBED

The cabbie dropped Jack off in the yard of the Pilipy's home.

"Hang around, will you?" Jack asked.

"Okay," the cabbie stated.

The house was an old two-story colonial affair with a stone foundation, wooden frame, gingerbread siding, and two brick chimneys. It appeared to have been recently painted a light blue with white trim. The porch stood out – stark white, overhang supported by ten equally spaced white wooden pillars.

The air was tepid, a late spring feeling with the odor of freshly cut grass drifting in the breeze. Jack went up the wooden steps under the shadow of the overhang and tried the doorknob. It was unlocked.

The old house reeked of dust and age. Sunlight was cascading through the cracks in the curtains. It fell in shafts that illuminated columns of floating dust. Old furniture was covered in gray sheets, by the stairs, was an oil lamp fitted with a Tiffany shade made up of yellow, red, and green stained glass.

Jack unbuttoned his tweed jacket and felt for the grip of his pistol. He approached the large lead framed plate-glass windows and pulled the drapes open.

A flood of golden light rushed in, and the room's neglected walls and high roof blazed with the dark colors of the Nineteenth Century's green and gold wallpaper.

Jack went around the bottom floor, opening windows in each room until the downstairs was awash with sunlight. Creaking echoed from above. A grunt drifted down from the stairs, and more creaking came.

"Who's up there?" demanded Jack.

The sound of footsteps on the stairs came further down. He pulled forth his pistol. "Who are you? Declare yourself – I'm an officer of the law!"

"What do you seek here?" a male voice asked. The footsteps retreated up the stairs.

Jack moved to the base of the steps. He looked up into the consuming darkness. In the black, a shape was apparent – like that of a person outlined in the upper hall.

"Who are you? Are you York?" demanded Jack.

"Check the top step – there you will see. Then, find the seascape. Behind it is the link you wish to find."

Jack took to the stairs. A scream filled the air. Something came down unnaturally fast.

The face – the twisted expression of agony was glowing in a white mist. Jack raised his pistol and fired. A bitter cold washed over him, and he fell back. He was immersed in a cold sweat as he hit the ground. The stairs were empty. He rolled and came up with his back to the wall and his pistol outstretched. There was no one.

The creaking was back upstairs.

"Come – it must be known. I cannot rest until the truth is told. Seek me under the floor…" came the voice again.

The front door flew open. The cabbie was there.

"Sir – I heard a shot! Are you okay?"

Jack looked at the fellow. "Mostly," Jack replied. "Stay down here. I have to check something." He went up the stairs. At the top, he examined the first step. It was slightly discolored. He ran his finger over it. "Oily," he said. He came back down. "Search each room for any picture of the ocean," he ordered the driver.

"Okay… but the gunfire?" the cabbie asked.

"That was me," Jack stated. "I'm a law enforcement agent looking for a missing person. There was someone else in the house. Now they're gone. Look for the image of the ocean. It's somewhere in this house."

A few minutes passed. The driver called from a back room.

"There's a mural of the coast in here."

Jack came. Indeed, the office's whole wall was an impressive painting of a beach with a sea cave, a radiant white moon in the upper corner, and a ship riding the dark waves.

"He was a hell of an artist," Jack said.

"What's this all about?" the cabbie asked.

"Not sure yet. Do me a favor and see if there is a basement door in the house. It might be covered by a rug or table. If not in the house, look outside—probably a door along the base of the foundation. Do not go in there. Come and get me when you find it." Jack turned back to the wall.

Running his hand over the picture, Jack noticed a slight crack along a lateral dark edge. This line met another nearly invisible one running vertically. He pressed, and a two-foot by two-foot door popped open.

There was a shelf with a strongbox hidden behind the panel. Taking it out, Jack put it on the desk by the window. It was locked.

"Officer – there's an access in the front room. It was hidden under the Persian rug and leads to the basement."

Jack went into the front room. The chairs were pulled back, and the rug was rolled up against the fireplace. He reached down for the recessed brass handle and pulled the door up and open.

Two wooden rods fell into slots in the floor to support the door. Stairs descended – sunlight from the room lighting the treads to the ground below. Jack went down a few steps and groped for a switch. A click – a dull glow from below drove away the remaining dark shadows.

"Should you go down there?" the cabbie asked.

Jack halted. He came back up. "Probably not." He looked around and found the telephone on the wall. Jiggling the switch, he got the operator. "Connect me with the sheriff."

Two sheriffs parked in the drive. They came up and entered the house.

"Where's Agent Parlance?" one of the men called - his

voice deep, filled with authority.

"Here," Jack said from the front room.

The two law enforcement officers came in. Jack was sitting on the raised hearth of the room's brick fireplace. He stubbed out his Black Cat and stood up.

"What's this all about?" one of the men asked.

"It's about murder, and that -" Jack pointed into the open basement access.

"You're Parlance? I'm Sheriff Doggerland." He held out his hand, and Jack shook it.

"I'm not sure what to make of it – but it's undeniable there was something bad going on here."

Doggerland nodded. "Shep – let's take a look." The two officers went into the basement. A moment later, they came back up. "Holy shit…" Doggerland stated. "I don't know what to say."

"Pilipy was a busy man," Jack told Doggerland.

The other officer suddenly shivered. "Felt like someone walked over my grave," he said.

"I felt it too," the cabbie said.

Jack nodded. "Some queer shit going on here. Is there someone in town who does photography?"

Doggerland looked surprised. "What?"

"A professional photographer with lights and such? I want this place documented."

"Who are you again?" Doggerland asked.

Jack showed him his badge. "I'm with the D.C. Bureau of Investigation. I'm looking for a missing kid – disappeared from New York. I hope that isn't him down there."

"Me too," Doggerland stated then turned to the cabbie. "Larry, why don't you go into town and fetch Billy Conner." Doggerland turned back to Jack. "He's the local photography expert." He turned around to Larry. "Bring him and his camera equipment out here straight away."

The cabbie seemed relieved to leave. "Okay, Paul. Glad to get the hell out of here. Back in a jiffy to drop off Bill."

"So, how the hell did you know to look down here?" Doggerland asked.

"There's a pattern in my investigation. Something to do with underground rituals and ancient rights." Jack drew in the smoke from his cigarette. He blew it out into the room. "I'll need to know from your coroner if the stiff's dental work matches my missing person." Jack handed Doggerland a card. "Have him send the results and the X-rays of the dead man's teeth here."

Doggerland nodded and put the card into his shirt pocket. "Damn bizarre. Heads in jars, bodies wrapped like presents…"

"Not presents," Jack said. "Egyptian mummies."

Doggerland chuckled. "You must be joking."

"For some reason, the killer was trying to make a mummy." Jack took out another Black Cat, took the nearly finished stub of his cigarette, and lit the new with the old. "Look, I don't pretend to understand what the hell is going on – but I do know what I've found during this investigation. I think it might be a cult – a group of people worshiping Egyptian gods."

Doggerland shook his head. "Only devout Christians in these parts," he said defensively.

Jack nodded to the basement door. "Not all."

* * *

The clock on the wall showed 2:23 p.m. Jack drank down the black coffee from a stained white porcelain mug. Sheriff Doggerland was on the phone with the local undertaker.

"Okay – I'll let him know. Thanks, Jerry. Ya, awful disturbing it is," the sheriff said, then hung up the phone.

"Hey, Sheriff? Mind if I use your phone?" Jack asked.

"Not in the least. If you're calling long distance, I assume the guys in D.C. will pay for the charges?"

Jack cracked a smile. It was everywhere he went – someone wanted something from the Feds, but they did not want the Feds. "I'll cover it."

He took up the receiver and tapped the terminator a couple of times. The local operator responded.

Jack blew out smoke from his nose. "I want a person-to-person connection to the Lucerne Hotel in Manhattan." There was a pause. "Ah – yes, the person. Connect me to the manager on duty there." A few minutes elapsed as Jack smoked and looked out the window onto Ulster Park's main street.

"Yes – is this the Lucerne in Manhattan? Good! I'm staying there – my name is Jack Parlance. Yes, the guy from Washington. I'm calling to check to see if there are any messages for me."

Doggerland was by a desk with his nose in an encyclopedia. He looked up and met Jack's stare, then looked back into the book.

"Three messages? I need you to tell me what they are. Okay – from D.C. H.Q. And the others? Doctor Xavier Blake. Information on the constellations and more. And the last message? Brenda McFadden. Okay. Give me the return number for Doctor Blake." Jack wrote down a number. "Thanks. I'll be calling again in a couple of hours." He hung up the receiver.

"Good news?" Doggerland asked.

"Not entirely." Jack picked up the receiver again and jiggled the terminator. "Yes, get me New York, Manhattan, Brown 14586." He took the cigarette from his mouth and put it with the burning side hanging over the phone box. "Hello? I'm calling for Doctor Blake. No – not black – I said, Blake. B.L.A.K.E – Blake." Jack was nearly shouting into the phone. "Yes – I'll wait." A few minutes passed. "Doctor Blake? I'm Agent Parlance from the Washington Bureau of Investigation. Yes – I'm the one who asked for information on the star patterns. I should be back in Manhattan by five. Okay – I look forward to your impressions."

Jack took the cigarette and drew in – then exhaled. "If

you don't mind me asking Doctor, are you an astronomer? No – a psychiatrist? Why would a psychiatrist be answering an astronomy question? Ah… indeed… I see… Yes – I'll find the place." Jack took out his notebook and scrawled down some information. "Very good. I'll see you soon." He hung up.

"If you're interested, the undertaker had some interesting news," Doggerland said. He took out a bottle of whiskey from the desk and two glasses. Putting them on the table, he poured half a glass each.

Jack came over and sat down. "So, what's the rumpus?"

"I talked with our coroner, Jerry March, and he told me that the body was wrapped in cloth like the type made in these parts twenty years ago. There's still piles of the stuff at the old factories along the river. He said the cadaver was in his forties, and most likely a farmhand or a drifter."

"So not my missing person," Jack said.

"Not your missing person – but someone's missing person," Doggerland stated.

"I need to head back to the city. But I plan on coming back in a day or so. I'll call. I'd like to have another look in that basement, then I want you to take me up to those old factories if you and a deputy have the time?" Jack stubbed out his smoke in the ashtray on the table. He hoisted the glass of alcohol to his lips and downed it. "Watch for a pair of tall, lanky fellows wearing white straw hats. They've been dogging my heels for a few days now. They claim to be officials – but I'm not so sure."

Doggerland nodded. "If they come out here, we'll find out exactly who they are."

"Can I get a lift to the train station?" Jack asked.

"Sure – don't mind helping out a fellow lawman," Doggerland said with a smile.

CHAPTER 11
ALLIES IN ORDER

Manhattan was as busy as ever. Jack made straight for the university. There he found the office of Xavier Blake. The man's office was cluttered with books, artifacts, and papers.

"Mister Parlance?" Blake said as Jack came into the room.

"Doctor Blake – I presume?" Jack said.

Blake chuckled as he shook Jack's hand. "The old Livingstone thing. I do appreciate a man with humor." He sat back down.

"So, why are you involved, Doctor Blake? I asked for an astronomer to look at the pattern and not a psychiatrist."

Blake took out a couple of cigars and offered Jack one. Jack took it and struck up a match. Blake ignited his and puffed on the end of his tobacco roll until the end was cherry-red.

"The request asked if the pattern was related to a star constellation. It is – it's Orion's Belt. The picture looks like it was taken in a Pharaoh's tomb. Did it originate from a tomb?"

"No – I had a photographer take it just a couple of days ago in a small room in the basement of a building here in town," Jack said.

"Really?" Blake drew in the dark smoke and blew it out into the room.

"You haven't answered my question, Doctor," Jack stated.

"I have some firsthand knowledge of Egyptian tomb art. This image is exactly like the one I saw when in Egypt in nineteen and one. I was part of an expedition investigating the funeral rites of the ancients, their book of the dead, and the effects of that model on the current modern psyche."

"What did you find?" Jack asked.

Blake took out a book and handed it to Jack. "Take a look at page one hundred and seven."

Jack thumbed through, found the page, and nodded. "The same type of picture of Orion's Belt," he said.

"Exactly. We found it in the burial site of Ny-Hor. They had dug down into solid bedrock, then capped the thing with a single slab of granite. The whole place was painted with that the most amazing colors and images."

"Who did you travel with?" Jack asked.

"I was part of a study team from the university. There was me, Doctor Frauhafer, Doctor Mead, Doctor Lester, Professor Carl Hersh, and Doctor Daisy Milkor." Blake blew more smoke up into the roof.

"Frauhafer?" Jack asked.

"Yes. He and I were the attending psychiatrists at the asylum on Ward's Island during the turn of the century. After we went to Egypt, Frauhafer invited me to his private residence along the coast in Maine to discuss a partnership. I declined to partner," Blake said.

"Why?" Jack asked.

"His theories were unconventional. His medical approach to treating those mentally afflicted was barbaric. When we returned from Africa, his use of the book of the dead as a guide was unethical. I reported his behavior as soon as I returned to New York," Blake said. "Now, you send the university this picture of a place – one that I witnessed and tell me that the picture was taken in a Manhattan building. This worries me."

"Worries you?" Jack asked.

"Frauhafer was convinced that those suffering schisms of consciousness saw into another reality. He believed that such a vision came when one was traumatized. If enough trauma can be incurred, it can break the boundary between this reality and another," Blake said.

"So, he's mad?" Jack puffed a smoke ring into the air over the desk.

Blake shook his head. "Because a person has abnormal beliefs does not make them crazy, Agent Parlance. But it can make them dangerous."

"Frauhafer is dangerous?"

"I'd hoped the sanctions from the medical board would have curbed his fantastic theories. It appears they might not have. Where did you have these pictures taken?"

"In a hidden chamber at the Asch Building." Jack eyed Blake.

Blake sat back. He was deep in thought. A minute passed in silence, then Blake spoke. "That's the place where those women were killed. Have you investigated the origin of the room? Was it part of the original structure or added later?"

"Original to the foundation. The architect confirmed it," Jack said.

"Then Frauhafer has been meddling in the occult far longer than I suspected," Blake stated.

"The occult is becoming a theme within my investigation," Jack declared. "What do you know of it?"

Blake tossed another book onto his desk. Jack picked it up.

"You're the author," Jack announced.

"Yes, an in-depth study of spiritualism as it relates to traumatic events, and its relation to the occult," Blake stated. "It is intertwined with religion, faith belief-systems, fear of death, accounts from those who came close to death, ancient rites, and in many cases, ancient gods."

"Is that what I'm dealing with here, Doctor Blake? Cult murders and ancient gods?" Jack asked.

Blake suddenly looked uncomfortable – as if he'd said too much too soon. "Well, what I mean is that those who you've come across might be part of a secret society focused on occult rituals intended to make…" Blake frowned. "Make magic."

Jack cracked a smile. "Magic? Like real magic – wizards and witches and the sort?"

Blake opened a drawer in his desk and pulled out a bottle of whiskey and a glass. He looked around on his desk and found a coffee mug and set it next to the glass. Pouring the glass half full, he handed the libation to Jack, then poured some for himself.

"The difference between technology and magic, Agent Parlance, is a slim one." He cleared his throat. "We got to talking about my past so fast, I didn't ask what your investigation is about," Blake said.

"A missing person. A young man named Jody Dobbs. He vanished from his apartment in Manhattan, and his family wants to know what happened to him," Jack stated, then took a healthy sip of the whiskey. "This ain't no paint," he said, holding up the glass.

"I have a man in Montreal who imports it from Ireland." Blake sat back and smiled. "This damned Prohibition is a nuisance." He leaned forward and took up the mug and drank. "Do you think this man Dobbs is mixed up in the cult?"

Jack drank down the rest of his whiskey and puffed on the cigar. "Not as such. More like a victim. He was a trust fund boy, possibly homosexual, into sadomasochistic play. His friends were too. I think he met someone who lured him away and possibly killed him. For the pleasure of pain – he would have gone willingly," Jack said. "I have more pictures of the basement room. If you have the time, Doctor Blake, would you mind taking a look?"

"Pictures of what exactly?" Blake poured more whiskey into each glass.

"There were carvings on each wall of the eight-sided room," Jack said.

"You must mean seven unless there was a relief on the back of the door," Blake said.

Jack again cracked a smile. "Indeed, so. There were seven figures. The door did not have any symbol or figure on it."

"I'll take a look," Blake said. "Where are they?"

Jack put out the cigar in the ashtray, placing the remaining stub into his shirt pocket. "For later," he said. "The pictures are at my hotel. If you would indulge me, I am quite able to buy dinner – on Uncle Sam's dime, of course."

Blake chuckled. "Of course. Okay – let's go. I'm very curious as to what those pictures will tell us."

"Us?" Jack asked.

"Unless I'm mistaken, you will require an expert in this area. I have the time, and a keen interest to see where this leads to." Blake stubbed out his cigar and stood up.

Jack stood too. "Alright, let's go."

The ride to the Lucerne did not take long. Blake waited in the lobby while Jack went up. Once back, he handed a manila envelope with the pictures in it to Blake.

"Interesting. These are the animal-headed gods of the Egyptians. Ah – the Free Mason's emblem. They are a secretive group. But, they're not pagans."

"What do you make of it?" Jack asked.

"Orion overhead. Seven ancient Egyptian gods. The tunnel and door leading into the room. It's the pathway of the afterlife, all right. There, one faces the challenge of the gods and their demons before you can reach the place we would call paradise," Blake said.

Jack flipped out a Black Cat and offered the Doctor one. The man shook his head.

"So, what does it mean?" Jack asked.

"Symbolic of the afterlife. Each one of these gods has a particular purpose. Here you have Nekhbet – god of the gates to the afterlife. Here is Sobek, the god of eternal life. Here is Set – the god of violence and chaos. This one is Horus – god of the sky. Aker is the god of the Earth. This is Hesat – the maternal goddess. The last one is Sekhmet – the destroyer." Blake laid each picture out on the cocktail table between the couches. "Curious indeed."

Jack sat back.

"I have to go back upstate tomorrow. I'm going to extend my stay for a few days. If you accompany me, I'd appreciate it. I believe I can also get you some scratch for your trouble, too," Jack said.

Blake smiled. "How could I resist? Shall I meet you at the station?"

"Yes. I have an 8:30 a.m. ticket to Ulster Park," Jack told him.

"I'll stop by the station on my way home and get a ticket. I'll meet you at 8:00 a.m. by the newsstand opposite the ticket office," Blake told Jack.

Jack slept hard. There were no ghosts, no nightmares, no bad thoughts. His sleep was dreamless – a dark void absent any meaning or feeling. When he woke, he felt rested and took a half-hour to shower, shave, and dress.

Once at the train station, he sought out Blake, who was by the newsstand. They boarded the train and settled in for a two-hour ride north. Halfway through the trip, they ate breakfast in the dining car and made polite conversation.

The train slid into Ulster Park Station at 10:30 a.m. Jack and Blake found their way to the sheriff's office. Doggerland took two deputies, and they all headed out to the Pilipy house. Once inside, Blake and Jack went downstairs into the musty cellar.

Blake went over to a raised platform topped with a slab of granite. "The body was here?"

Jack nodded. "All wrapped like one of those mummies Carter found."

"And, there were jars – some made of glass with heads in them, and some made of pottery with organs in them?" Blake asked.

"Yes," Jack replied as he popped a Black Cat into his mouth and lit it.

Blake picked up a roll of leather and unfurled it on the table. Copper blades and metal hooks appeared in small pouches inside.

"Torture devices?" Jack asked.

"No – embalming tools. The same types were used by the ancient Egyptians. Odd about the heads in jars. The ancient Egyptians didn't do that sort of thing." Blake took out the long probe-like hook. "This was used to break into the brain cavity and scramble the brain, then allow it to drain through the nose of the deceased."

Jack blew smoke into the room. "Sounds gruesome," he stated.

Blake went to a workbench. He opened some drawers and looked on shelves. Taking a few items, he put them on the embalming table.

"Look here. These are modern carved reliefs of the Egyptian gods. Part of the Pharos Book of the Dead." Blake looked up at Jack, then his eyes drifted over his shoulder. "What's that?"

Jack turned and saw a wall bathed in shadow and drawings. "I'll be damned if I know."

Blake came over. "Give me your flashlight?"

Jack handed it over.

The illumination showed a six-inch circle of light on top of various depictions of gods, monsters, and conveyances such as boats and chariots, intermixed were hieroglyphs.

"Look!" Blake was reverent and excited. "The journey begins here." He ran his finger along each cell containing information. "A body is prepared in a sacred way in this image. Then, the soul leaves the body here. He travels to the underworld. A demon meets him and challenges the deceased. He must be protected by a spell – to allow him not to be consumed, he then speaks the magic – to defend himself, and gain entry into the tunnels. The newly dead goes upon a reed boat through the water, and there are more challenges here, here, and here."

Blake moved along the wall. "Here, he exits the underworld and is born into the sky realm. From there, he will board the sun-ark and travel to meet Osiris back in the underworld. There - his heart will be weighed, and if found light, he will be admitted into the universe to join in ruling all of existence. If his heart is heavy – regret, misdeeds, cruelty, and neglect – he will be either sent back to the world to repent, or if his sins are sufficiently terrible, his soul will be torn apart and sent into oblivion."

Jack took a long drag from his cigarette. "So, what the hell does this have to do with this murder or my case?"

Blake returned to the table and looked over the items. "Here is a symbol that is not Egyptian… it's Sumerian. And, this one… it is Hittite… I think." He held up a three-inch medallion. "This is old. Look at the image." He handed it to Jack.

"Some kind of snake-headed monster," Jack said.

"Odd, and yet fits in with the animal deities of the ancients." Blake put the medallion into his pocket. "I'll see if a colleague can give us a better view of what this is."

Jack nodded, then led the way back up into the house. He excused himself and went into the back room and retrieved the strongbox from the hidden chamber.

"What's that?" Blake asked.

"Not sure yet," Jack said. But I'll soon find out."

CHAPTER 12
INDRID COLD

Jack, Blake, and the officers arrived back at the sheriff's office just after noon. Jack called in his report to D.C., and Blake called his friend from the university. Afterward, they went to a diner and had lunch.

"My friend wants me to bring the amulets to him immediately," Blake said. "I'll take the next train back to the city."

"Alright," Jack confirmed. "I'll head out to the old weaving mills and have a look around." Jack glanced at Blake. "Don't get yourself killed. There are some who appear to want all this put to bed, and they're not afraid of killing to do it."

Blake chuckled. "I'll be on my guard."

After lunch, Blake left on the 2:30 p.m. train for Manhattan. Jack and the sheriff's men picked out some weapons from the locker and began driving up to the old river mills.

Thunder echoed in the distance as heavy black clouds began to cluster overhead. The animals grew quiet as the over-ripe droplets of water fell from the sky. A wind blew from the east, and the bluster grew in intensity.

By the time they parked along the old road by the mills, the sky was black with clouds, and the light was like that of the early evening. In the driving rain and howling wind, there seemed unintelligible voices.

"Okay," Doggerland began. "Bill, you and Alexander head around back. Jack and I will cover the front. Don't shoot each other!"

Bill chuckled. "Don't worry boss, we got it handled." Bill turned on his flashlight.

The two sheriffs took up their shotguns and moved through the tangled brush and brambles around the back toward the river.

"Looks like it's you and me," Doggerland said.

"Before we head in there, give a call to your office. You may want to have a couple more men sent out here," Jack suggested.

Doggerland thought for a moment, then he nodded. "I feel uneasy about this too. Okay." He picked up the transmitter and sent the message. The office replied, and two more men were dispatched.

An unearthly glow emitted from the cracks in the walls of the dark red brick. The roof was more than three stories high, and the sheet metal roof was roaring with the bacon-sizzling sound of the rain. Bountiful streams poured off the top, landing on the cobblestone surrounding the building.

Jack approached a wooden side-door. There was no handle on the weathered surface, just a dirty rope protruding from a rough-cut hole in the face.

He listened – then gently pulled the rope. A subtle click – barely audible - rose in the air. He pushed, and the blockage silently swung inward. All-consuming freezing darkness lay beyond.

Jack entered the silent structure. He brought up the Thompson and carefully felt with his foot for any debris or obstruction that lay before him. He took a step. Silently Doggerland closed the door behind them.

Jack's eyes adjusted. A faint and nearly imperceptible light illuminated the narrow hall roofed with black tarpaper and floored with slate blocks.

As quietly as he could move, Jack came to a doorframe absent a door. Beyond, he saw the interior of the warehouse. The glow from lanterns cast a primitive luminance. Lines of sacks hung from broad beams up in the roof.

"Giant figs?" Doggerland whispered.

Jack was silent. He pointed up above at the dozen blazing lanterns dangling from the wooden roof. Taking another step, Jack stopped and pointed at the wires running from white porcelain insulators nailed into the wall. Doggerland nodded.

The absence of sound was deafening. Jack slowly moved from the doorway and across the cement floor to the nearest pear-shaped bag. Doggerland followed.

A desperate scream came from far off. Jack remained still – listening – waiting. The sack shifted slightly. Jack peered into the partially transparent bag. His eyes involuntarily went wide, and a panicked chill ran up his spine. There was a face – a human face looking back – the eyes in a state of terror and agony – almost pleading.

Doggerland looked, then stumbled backward, hitting a sawhorse with some boards.

Jack stepped away, his skin crawling with a sense of abject horror.

A half dozen shots echoed from outside. Then came a scream. Jack moved quickly down the line of hanging sacks – then stopped abruptly where the bags ended, and an open space began. It looked like an operating theater.

Doggerland put his hand on Jack's shoulder and pointed. A behemoth of a man was stomping toward the table with a body in his arms.

A man, nearly as large as Jack stood with his back to him. On the table was laid one of the sheriff's deputies. His arms and legs were broken, and his head turned as if looking for help – any help.

The flash of a metal saw appeared, and the mad surgeon prepared to cut.

"Stay where you are!" shouted Jack as he leveled the Thompson at the man. "Put the blade down and turn around!

Slowly, the arm with the saw lowered, setting the instrument on the table. Then, he turned around. Jack took two steps backward, bumping into Doggerland, who gasped loudly. Jack's hand began to shake. The thing had no nose, no lips, and its eyes were coal-black. The dark brown leather apron it wore was stained with blood and what appeared to be several bullet holes in it.

It was coming for Jack. Almost without conscious thought, Jack squeezed the trigger and unleashed the fury of one hundred 45 caliber rounds in a hailstorm of firepower.

The bullets tore into the abomination, punching dark holes through that leather smock. Yet, the thing kept coming.

Snapping shut, the bolt on the long gun halted. The barrel sizzled, and the magazine expired.

The creature latched its hands around Jack's throat. He hit the thing in the face, but it was immovable. Using all his strength, he drove his fist into the right arm of the beast and loosened the thing's grip.

Jack drove forward, and the monster stumbled. He pushed both his hands upward between the creature's arms and stepped to the side – the grip was broken, and Jack pulled forth his pistol and fired point-blank into the monster's face. It fell back and hit the ground hard – and didn't get up.

Jack heard a clicking sound. He turned and saw Doggerland with his revolver out extended at arm's length – his finger reflexively pulling the trigger though all the cartages were spent.

The cordite smoke was clearing, and Jack's heart pounded hard in his chest. He looked down at the monster, pointed his pistol at the creature's head, and fired another round. Turning back to Doggerland, he walked over, took hold of the revolver, and laid his hand on Doggerland's arm.

"It's over," Jack said. "It's okay now."

Doggerland relinquished his firearm and looked at Jack, then down at the body of the giant mad man. "What in God's name…"

"The deputy!" Jack shouted, then turned and rushed to the man on the table, only to find he'd bled out. The contorted form - arm bones and leg bones had pierced his skin, and the deputy was pale as ash and stone dead.

"It's Bill," Doggerland said, coming alongside. He seemed in shock. "What about Alexander?"

Moving quickly through the warehouse, they found a door leading to the riverside of the property. The other sheriff was lying there, his back snapped like a twig, and his head turned around facing backward.

A clap of thunder filled the air. A bright light blasted from within the building.

"You have killed my surgeon," a faint voice called from inside the structure.

Jack spun around his pistol at the ready. "Come on," he said to Doggerland.

As they reached the door, all the white light vanished from the warehouse, and it fell back into the soft glow of the lanterns.

The two men stopped at the surgery table.

"Your kind is curious, but not very smart. Would you like to see what I have created? There must be suffering – and suffering is a wonderful tonic."

A shadow moved near the sacks. Jack and Doggerland found their arms and legs frozen in place as the dark figure approached. The stranger stepped out from behind one of the fig-sacks. In his hand was a cylinder with copper tubes with wires hanging off.

He was nearly as tall as Jack, had no hair upon his head, and his eyes were much further apart than an average person's.

He stood like an actor on a stage and bowed slightly. Jack saw his face was abnormal, for the sides of his mouth went up along his cheeks as if someone had sliced them up to his ears. He smiled a mouth full of white teeth, then clicked his jaws together, making a snapping sound.

"Here – look upon this suffering as a gift and a portent I give you," the man said, and went to a set of knife-edge switches by the operating table and closed several.

A collection of agonizing screams rose as the sacks

twisted and shook. Jack could only look on as sparks spit and fell around.

The thing threw back its head and, with a maniacal laugh, chattered its teeth together. Then, it opened the switches and came closer to Jack and Doggerland. The horrible screams from the sacks slowed and then stopped. Only an occasional whimpering could be heard as a feeling of horror hung in the air.

"Ahh… now that was good!" The man sniffed around Jack and Doggerland. "I am not unfamiliar with the taste of cooked man flesh. We love it so. It was once a delicacy in my land but is being replaced by other pleasures."

He came full circle around the two frozen lawmen. "I love the taste almost as much as using you to experiment on. You do not feel pain as we do – and that interests me," he said. "Also, you are not half as intelligent as we, and that makes your brains ripe for dissecting."

Jack was desperately trying to move. His muscles were locked - burning, his eyes straining.

"You will make the most splendid agony sack. Yes – of all my pain-bags, I think I will cherish you most of all. Don't worry, in two clicks of my jaws, I'll have those arms and legs off, and you comfortably in a sack. Now sleep agent Parlance – and dream of the war that you so rudely failed to die in." He raised his hand. In it was a glass syringe with a long needle.

Jack suddenly found his hands clutching the monster's neck. He pushed forward as the thing tried to stab him with the syringe. Jack punched with all his might at the distorted face. The thing fell back, hit the surgery table, tumbled about, then fled toward the door.

Taking up his pistol, Jack fired at the thing. The echo of a ricochet filled the air, there was a flash of fire – one of the oil lanterns in the ceiling burst. The upper structure was on fire.

"We will meet again – I will come for you," the thing said as it vanished out the far door. "I will find you as easily as a dog finds a bone!"

Fire was consuming the structure. Jack choked, grabbed Doggerland, and staggered toward the nearest door. The sacks were twisting and undulating. The fire was sweeping through the space quickly. There would be no salvation for any left inside.

Stumbling outside, the rain was coming down hard. The yellow flames of the fire licked out through the disintegrating brick walls and buckling roof.

Creaking and popping came from the building. Jack looked all around the grounds – that thing was out there – somewhere.

He finally stopped and dropped Doggerland to the muddy ground. The man scrambled up against the car and curled up into a fetal position.

Reaching into his shirt pocket, Jack pulled out his pack of Black Cats and stuck one into his mug. Covering the end, he lit it, then inhaled deeply.

"What the God damned hell is going on?" Jack said into the dark rainy night.

In the distance, Jack heard ringing bells. A short while later, the siren of a fire truck grew close. Jack waited for the authorities and the fire department. He wanted to know how many people were killed – or was it all just a horrible nightmare? Would he wake up in the hotel? How could such things be real?

Headlights illuminated the street. The fire was bathing all the other buildings in a harsh orange glow. A police car arrived, and two men got out. One saw Jack and approached.

"Agent Parlance? Where is the Sheriff, Bill, and Alexander?"

"The Sheriff is over there by the car," Jack said flatly. "Bill was inside. Alexander's body is around the back.

"What happened?" the officer asked.

"Madmen, and maniacs," Doggerland yelled in a sudden fit. "I couldn't move – its face – its face – a nightmare!

"What happened here?" the deputy pressed Jack.

Doggerland again shouted. "He'll kill us, he said so. That thing – those people... Burning, screaming, the screams!"

The deputies restrained the Sheriff. He was growing more agitated as he looked around into the shadows of the night.

"What the God damned hell happened here?" demanded the deputy.

"Murder, and something far more horrible. Nothing like I've ever seen before," Jack said as he sat down on the bumper of the Sheriff's car. "To be completely honest – I don't know what the hell is going on here."

CHAPTER 13
NERVES A JANGLED

Jack entered the sheriff's office just after 7 p.m. He sat in the first chair he came to, leaned forward, and put his face into his hands. The evening had stimulated some part of his mind – that part leftover from the war – the part he wanted to shut away.

The deputy came over with a bottle of whiskey and set out a few cups. He poured liberal amounts into each and handed one to Jack.

"Look," the deputy began. "I want to know what the hell happened out there, and I want to know it now. There are two men dead, and the sheriff is out of his mind. You're barely hanging on by a thread, it seems to me, and before you go over, I want your side of the story."

Jack put the strongbox on the desk next to him. He drank down the whiskey and indicated he wanted more. The deputy obliged.

It was an odd thing. Though Jack could hear the deputy's question, he also heard Maxim machine gunfire in the background. There was also the terrifying whistle from artillery shells. He was slipping back – the darkness of the war was closing in around him, and he was nearly ready to start punching wildly and rushing from the building – scream into the sky – shout at God and the devil!

"Agent Parlance?" the deputy shouted.

All the background sounds stopped. He was again sitting in a building in a small town in Upstate New York.

"Find me a small skeleton key," Jack said.

The deputy nodded, left, and returned with the key. Jack took it and opened the box. There were notebooks, documents, and a small number of stock shares.

"Listen," Jack started. "What happened back there… I'm trying to get my head around it. We arrived just as the rain began. We found a building filled with bags that held people. Bill and Alex were murdered by a giant madman. I unloaded a whole drum of 45 rounds into him – and he kept coming. I'm not sure if it was my pistol shot that killed the thing, or Doggerland's, but one of us finally got him."

Jack drank down the second whiskey, then took the bottle. "We found one of the deputies around the back – broken like a man breaks kindling. The other… Bill, I think was his name, he was going to be butchered…" Jack stopped. "I'm a little out of sequence. We found Bill first, then Alex. Then, there was this person with a grotesque face. He sent electricity into those bags - the bags had people in them. They screamed and twisted." Jack visibly shivered.

The deputy poured more alcohol into Jack's glass.

"That person was torturing innocent people in those sacks. He tried to kill Doggerland and me. We were frozen – couldn't move for some reason. He was coming for us. I don't know how – but I got my hands around its neck, and we fought. He ran – I fired after him. One of the lanterns in the ceiling exploded, and the place burned down." Jack stopped. He felt he was rambling. Looking up, he saw four young deputies staring back at him, two with mouths agape.

From the back cell, Doggerland began screaming. "He's coming for me! He's coming – in the darkness!"

"Go get Doc. Howard. Tell him to come quick," the deputy told another.

Jack drank down the remaining libation and stood.

"You'd better bring more booze too," Jack told the young man. "Now – I have to make a call." He went directly to the telephone and lifted the receiver. "Connect me to Washington D.C. person-to-person to the Bureau of Investigation, from Jack Parlance for William J. Flynn."

* * *

Jack entered the Lucerne Hotel lobby. He had spent hours on the train coming back from Ulster Park, and his nerves were raw. Approaching the counter, he asked if there were any messages.

"Three, sir," the young clerk said.

Jack took the notes and read them. One was from Flynn – an urgent request that he visit the location of a mansion in Whitehall, New York, owned by a Doctor Theodore Sachs. The second was from Blake asking him to contact him as soon as he was in. The third was from McFadden – she stated a "mutual acquaintance" with a white hat had contacted her and Jimmy. She wanted to see Jack ASAP.

Ringing the elevator, Jack waited. When the doors opened, he stepped in and told the young operator the floor. The lift moved upward.

Once in his room, he tapped for the operator. "Get me…" he paused to look at the note, "Bryant 9675, please." A moment passed, then there was a ring. "Doctor Blake? It's Agent Parlance. Yes. You did? Okay. I have to head up to Whitehall, New York. A lead from headquarters."

He looked at his watch. "I'm going to catch a few hours of sleep. Meet you in the lobby of my hotel in four hours." He hung up and jiggled the terminator.

"Operator? Get me Murry Hill 3993. Thank you." He waited. "Jack Parlance for Brenda McFadden. Jack said. "Who? Jimmy? Okay – Jimmy, it's Jack Parlance. What happened? They did? You did what? Well, that will keep 'em at arm's length for a while." Jack chuckled. "Bring Brenda and meet me in the lobby of my hotel in four hours. Okay – not to worry." He hung up, climbed into bed, set the clock alarm, and fell into a deep sleep.

* * *

In the morning, Jack stepped out of the elevator into the lobby. Sitting on the couch was Brenda and Jimmy, and across from them in a chair was Doctor Blake.

"Good – you're all here," Jack said.

Brenda looked at Blake and only then realized she knew the man. She smiled and extended her hand to Blake.

"Doctor Blake," she said.

"A pleasure to see you again, Ms. McFadden."

Jimmy came over. "Jim McKerry," he said and shook Blake's hand.

"Okay – we've all met each other." Jack cleared his throat. "Tell me what happened?" he asked Brenda.

She sat back down. "We had a visit from two men in white straw hats. They tried to strong-arm me – Jimmy and a few of my boys told them to take it on the heel. There was a little ruckus, and they were showed the door – but one said they were coming back."

"Did they?" Jack asked.

"They somehow came into my room while I was preparing to sleep. I shot one, but it didn't seem to knock him down." Brenda visibly shuddered. "They tried to grab me and cut me with a razor, but Jimmy came in and shot both – they stopped and fled. But there was no blood. How can that be?"

"Are you sure you hit them?" Blake asked.

"Of course!" Jimmy replied. "Two rounds each."

"Okay – set yourself up in a safe house somewhere and send word to me –"

Brenda cut Jack off. "Look federal flat-foot – I'm not leaving your side until you get those yeggs off me or they get ventilated. Those guys are shaking down my business, and I don't like it!"

Jack looked at Blake, who cracked a smile. "They could come in handy if things get daffy," Blake said.

Taking out a Black Cat, Jack lit it and thought for a few moments. "Okay, you can come with me and the doc. Don't get in the way, and if I pull my firearm, make sure you're behind me and hit the deck," Jack told them as he spewed out the gray tobacco smoke into the lobby. "Hope you got some scratch cause you both got to pay your own way."

Brenda looked visibly relieved. "Music to my ears. We got enough simoleons to keep us in gin and tonic – and smokes." She took out a gold cigarette case, opened it, removed one, then waited for someone to light it.

Jimmy reached into his pocket, but Jack beat him to the punch, and Brenda's smoke blazed to life. She inhaled, then exhaled through her nose. "So, big fella – where we off to?"

Jack fought back a smile. "We're off to Whitehall Upstate. Hope you packed some sundries and clean undies."

Brenda chuckled. "Keep an extra set in the car at all times. Never know when one has to beat it out of town."

Jimmy was quiet. He watched the two interact, then looked over at Blake. "So, you're what kind of doctor?"

"Psychiatrist," Blake said.

"A Voodoo man – a head shrinker," Jimmy said with a morose chuckle. "If them fellas with the white straw hats come back, they're going to need a coroner, not a brain-shrinker."

Jack held Jimmy in his gaze. "Look – this is a police matter. We ain't killing for the sake of killing. This ain't the Somme or some back-alley shakedown. Got me?"

Jimmy nodded and remained quiet.

"Okay, let's get the hell out of here and on a train." Jack led the way, hailed a cab, and all five got in. "Take us to Grand Central," he ordered.

As the group traveled north, they drank coffee and ate pastries in the dining car while Jack laid out the case's facts.

"Jody was a freak," Brenda said as she lifted a bone-china cup to her lips and drank some coffee.

Jimmy shook his head. "His money was good – why care if he was a sodomite?"

"It's not that he was homosexual, it's the other stuff he did – his sadomasochistic fetishes. They may have led him to the cult, and this cult may have murdered him," Blake said.

"Poor kid," stated Brenda as she exhaled smoke into the ceiling of the car.

Jack looked out the window. The countryside was flying by. He fiddled with his cigarette as he stared.

"My colleague in the archeology department said these three amulets were not Egyptian, but some other culture – maybe Babylonian, Hittite, or some unknown one. Look at the images," Blake said as he put the items on the table.

One was an odd creature with a round head and wide-open mouth – like a cat yawning. The other depicted a centaur looking creature, but with four arms and a horse head and face. On the last was an octopus creature with a shrimp-like body.

Jack casually looked at them, then picked up his cup and drank some black coffee.

"This one – looks like the monster Doggerland and I met in the torture warehouse."

"Torture warehouse?" Brenda asked, sitting forward.

"Ya – a terrible thing I'd like to forget," Jack said.

"What about the items of the strongbox?" Blake asked.

Jack pulled up his leather satchel. "Several diaries, some documents, ring, money clip, diamond stickpin, and stocks." He poured out the contents onto the table.

Blake picked up a notebook. "William Flannery?" he asked. "I know him. He's locked up on Ward's Island."

"Really?" Jack asked.

"He was an army doctor during the Great War. His mind cracked. Kept yammering about some monstrous machine cracking open the walls and voices speaking from the other side. Unseen things coming to get him. If I remember correctly, his apartment was filled with books about spells and magic. He was a big spiritualist," Blake said.

"Look at this beetle," Brenda held up a dark blue pendant.

"A scarab," Blake corrected. "Used in Egyptian rituals for good fortune and protection of the soul."

"Whatever in the hell it is, can it be sold for some cash?" Jimmy asked.

"To a museum, maybe," Blake replied.

CHAPTER 14
UNWELCOMED NEWS

The train rattled to a halt in Whitehall Station. They exited the train and found a car to take them out to the Skene Manor.

A short while later, Jack saw the stark white stone walls of the house. The hilltop view from the property allowed a panorama perspective of Whitehall.

Construction crews were hard at work – some up on scaffolding, others coming and going from the house.

A cable was connected to a large clock face; it appeared ready to be hauled up the tower to fill a giant hole at the top.

A tall man with a broad jaw, narrow nose and dark blue penetrating eyes came from the front door.

"Can I help you?" the man asked.

Jack introduced himself and noted his companions as colleagues. The man finished wiping his hands with a rag and shook each person's hand.

"I'm Theodore Sachs. I'm the local doctor in these parts. What business do you have with me?"

Jack took out his pack of Black Cats, put one into his mouth. "I'm investigating the disappearance of a young man named Jody Dobbs. He hasn't been seen in quite some time, and his family fears he may have fallen victim to foul play." Jack lit his cigarette.

"What does this have to do with me?" Sachs asked.

"Did you know a William Flannery?" Jack blew dark gray smoke into the air.

"Bill Flannery? Major Flannery?" Sachs's voice was slightly shaken.

Jack looked up as the clock was lifted – inch by inch. "Yes."

"I knew him during the war. A competent surgeon…" Sachs' voice trailed off as if he was growing nervous. "You'd better come inside." He looked around the driveway.

Inside, Sachs ordered his housekeeper to fetch some coffee and pastries. He sat down on a couch in the lounge, and the others followed suit.

"Listen – I don't know what anyone has told you, but you shouldn't be asking about Bill. He… went mad."

"Why shouldn't we ask?" Blake's voice was even – modulated.

"Look – if they find out you came here, I'll be in danger. They said that we are not allowed to talk about what happened."

Jack casually drew in a lung of smoke and exhaled. "Who would hurt you? Who told you to keep quiet?"

Sachs looked worried as the coffee came, followed by a plate with cream-filled pastries. "You don't know what you're getting into. Just go and drop this investigation."

"Did you know a man named Jody Dobbs?" Jack asked.

"I've never heard of this person named Dobbs. I really must insist that you do not ask me about Bill, either. That person is long gone," Flannery stated.

"Now why would we do that," Brenda said as she reached for a cup of the black coffee and a pastry. She took a dainty bite and sip, then set them down again. "Mister Sachs – you've shown us such hospitality." She crossed her legs, and her flapper dress hung open at the intersection of her thighs. "Calm yourself and take a deep breath. Surely, there is no one here who will harm you. Agent Parlance has some questions, and they need to be answered."

Sachs looked around the room, then he sat back down, but his panic was still visible. "These people mean business."

"Just start with how you know William Flannery," Jack instructed.

Taking in a deep breath, Sachs seemed to calm a bit. "Well… I met Bill in 1916. We were army surgeons treating some of the most horrible wounds that man can inflict on another: amputations, bisections, brain surgery, and more.

"Flannery and I were approached in Paris by a Doctor Frauhafer, who was tasked by the Department of War and accompanied by two officers from the Office of Misadventure (OM) to help with some experiments. At first, we were directed to perform everyday operations and reconstructive surgeries. A few months later, we were taken to a French country home outside Paris, where we were required to conduct some very… unnatural works.

"After another couple of months – I couldn't bear what I was doing. Both Bill and I were being torn to shreds mentally by what they were asking us to do. Then, Frauhafer let us know we were being discharged, we got a large packet of money, and sent on a steamer home.

"Once back, we were separately visited by those men from the OM wearing white straw hats – expressionless – faces that haunt my dreams to this day. They made it clear that we would end up in a similar hospital, like the one we worked in, if we ever discussed what we did. That was threat enough for me." Sachs took up his cup of coffee and, with a shaking hand, drank some. "Flannery and I communicated for a couple of years, but he was growing more distance and muddled in the head. The last I heard from him was a year ago. He was rambling about Frauhafer and the magic he keeps in a cavern under his home in Maine. He must have been spying on the man."

"Frauhafer approached me as well," said Blake to Sachs. "You are quite out of his reach now. I take it the surgeries were unnecessary and revolting?"

Sachs nodded his head and drank some more coffee. "I'm sorry – I don't know this Dobbs person. But, if he was picked up by Frauhafer's people, he is most likely not human anymore – if he is still living."

"Flannery is in an asylum in New York," Blake said.

Sachs' face went pale. "My God – you have to get him

out of there. They'll…"

"What?" Jack pressed.

It was clear that Sachs was struggling. His mouth moved, but nothing came out. He again took up his coffee. "If you want any answers, there are two places you should look at. One is the Mercantile Meat Processing Plant (MMPP) in Pennsylvania. Their wagons were always there in France to clean up the remains of our work. The other is Frauhafer's estate in Maine. He calls it Grey Manor, up by Ashdale somewhere off of the Cox Head Road. Bill told me about it in one of his calls. I thought he was quite mad."

Blake nodded. "I know of it. The rail line ends at a town called Ashdale." He took out a cigar and put it into his mouth. "The area is quite remote. His house is on a cliff overlooking the Kennebec River inlet. I stayed there for two weeks many years ago. Very unsettling place."

"What about this Mercantile Meat Processing Plant in Pennsylvania?" Jack asked.

Sachs seemed more at ease. His eyes darted less around the room, and his manner became relaxed. "The MMPP was created to provide food for the fighting man in the American Civil War. They had some sort of special dispensation that made them forever exempt from taxes and all regulations set out by D.C. But they've been mostly forgotten."

"Never heard of it," Jimmy said.

"But, you've heard of Prodoo, and Kasgill, and Lorington foods?" Sachs asked.

All four nodded.

"Fronts for the MMPP. Early on, they took dying or injured animals, carcasses found on the streets of Chicago and New York, and other northern cities, and had them shipped by rail to the plant. There they processed the rotted stuff into food. They began to take the bodies of people, and other things – all processed into your favorite canned foods. During my stay at that French hospital, they took the rejects from the government's experiments – the ones that Frauhafer led, and turned them into your favorite sausage, or ground beef, or canned ham."

Brenda's face contorted. "You must be joking! You mean that humans were added to those brands?"

Sacks nodded his head solemnly. "During the war, many a dead and dying soldier were picked up by special ambulance teams and put into freezer cars, and on freezer ships, and sent to that coal-fired factory in Pennsylvania." He visibly shivered. "My God – what they have done. I've heard that the MMPP is run by a guy over a hundred years old. I doubt he is human, either. Somehow he became familiar with Frauhafer…"

"I want you to go make a statement. Write it down before we leave," Jack said.

Sachs nervously laughed. "Not on your life. Let me tell you something. When you leave, I'm going to lay awake at night with a pistol on my chest. I'll have five shots to get those bastards before they get me, then one for myself. I won't let them take me."

Jack nodded. "I'll keep your name out of my report. But, if push comes to shove, I'll have to bring you in. We can protect you if that happens."

"The hell you say!" Sachs said resolutely. "Once you leave, I don't want to see any of you again." He stood up and looked at the empty coffee cups and plates. "Now – I apologize for my abruptness, but please get the hell out of my house."

They left Skene Manor. The taxi was waiting. Jack looked back at the home. He saw someone peeking out from one of the windows, then retract – leaving the drapes to flutter slightly.

"He's scared shitless," Jimmy said as they got in, and the taxi began heading to Whitehall Station.

"With good reason," Blake stated. "Frauhafer is mad – and dangerous. He's obsessed with magic and death – and causing pain."

"Doctor, is Sachs mad?" Brenda asked.

"He might well be," Blake said.

"I'll go to Pennsylvania and see that MMPP place for myself," Jack said.

"We'll go too," Brenda told Jack, also volunteering Jimmy.

Jimmy shrugged his shoulders. "If we must. First, I want to stop by the club, pick a couple of things, and see if those white hat sons of bitches came back."

Blake smoked his cigar. "I'll go to, but I need to pick up my investigation kit from home before we leave. I suggest we get a wiggle on if we're to make the next train to Manhattan."

The taxi driver drove quickly to the station where they all caught the train. A couple hours later, they arrived at Grand Central – making their separate ways to taxis and slipping into the congestion of the coming evening.

CHAPTER 15
VOICES FROM THE DARK

Jack arrived back at his hotel. There were four messages. He thumbed through them.

One was from H.Q. Flynn thanked him for his report and wanted to know what he found in Upstate. The second was from James Fine, Doggerland's deputy. The note read that Doggerland was recovering, but was still being sedated. The next did not have a name but said that Jack should keep an eye out for a man called The Cardinal. The last was from the Lipton medical examiner, who had completed his report of the body found in the abandoned Manhattan house. The man had strangled himself while confined.

Jack headed for the lift. Up he went to his room and a change of clothes. He called hotel services and asked that his dirty clothes be laundered and left them outside the door in a bag.

His phone rang, and he picked it up. "Jack here," he said.

"It's Brenda. Those white-hatted bastards came back. A few of my boys caught one and worked him over. They locked him in a back room, and when they went to show me, he was gone. There was no way out of that room!"

"Try and grab some shuteye. Meet me in the lobby of my hotel tomorrow at five in the morning," Jack said.

"Okay. We'll see you there."

Jack hung up, lit up a smoke, then picked up the receiver again and dialed. He talked a few minutes with Blake - agreed to meet in the lobby, then hung up and laid down. He was tired – bone tired. Rolling over, he set the alarm, then closed his eyes. This time – his old comrades came to visit him on the dark and soggy battlefield.

The next morning, Jack met his companions in the hotel's foyer, then walked over to the clerk's desk and asked for any messages. There was one. The note was from Flynn – it said, "Determine if the company MMPP is involved. No stone unturned. Report back ASAP."

"We're headed to Pennsylvania," Jack declared. He made for the door and hailed a cab.

Grand Central Terminal was packed with travelers. Jack carried his satchel; Brenda had a medium-sized suitcase. Jimmy held a sailor's sea-bag and a leather case, and Blake brought what looked like a toolbox and a small bag.

The group wound their way through the newspaper boys, shoeshine stands, cigarette-gum girls, and the swarms of businessmen and women. Once their tickets were purchased, they made their way to the platform and onto the Pullman passenger car. Brenda, Jimmy, and Blake surrendered their luggage to a porter, while Jack carried his satchel on board.

They'd be on the train for the whole day. The ticket spelled out the destination time of 2:00 p.m. at Williamsport.

Jack took up a seat and set his satchel on the floor by his feet. Blake sat opposite, and Jimmy and Brenda sat across the aisle.

Twenty minutes later, the car lurched from the platform and began to ease out of the station heading west.

Just as they were clearing Trenton, Jack got up, picked up his case, and declared, "I'm off to the dining car." The others followed.

The men ordered – scrambled eggs, bacon, toast, and donuts. Brenda ordered half a grapefruit and toast. They all drank coffee and smoked afterward.

"What's so important in PA that we have to go now?" Brenda asked.

"My boss says I need to check out the MMPP. Oh – by the way, I've received a warning about someone called The Cardinal. Keep an eye out for anyone looking like an official of the Catholic church."

"This is all most exciting," Blake stated as he puffed away at his cigar.

"I just want to know what yeggs we need to... handle to get those white-hatted shit stains off our backs and away from our clubs." Jimmy declared.

Brenda nodded her head, solemnly. "Exactly. Also, I don't want them to kill us."

"I don't want anyone to get killed," Jack said as he took out his portfolio of documents. He handed the papers around. "Have a look. Let me know if you can make heads or tails out of this mess. I'm having a hell of a time." Jack sat back and put his pack of Black Cats on the table next to it his lighter. "Porter – more coffee," he called.

Slowly the documents made the rounds until everyone had seen them.

"I see that we were all mentioned in there," Blake said, his mouth forming a frown. "You didn't mention we were possible suspects."

Jack shrugged his shoulders. "It was pretty clear none of you are. This Frauhafer is, though, and now this place called the Mercantile Meat Processing Plant." He pulled out one last document in a manila envelope and handed it to Blake. "Have a look. What do you think?"

Blake reviewed the ten pages of typed information. "Remarkable," he finally said. "No accountability – and who is this Vladimir Peebles – he can't still be alive. I mean, he'd be over... a hundred and thirty years old."

Again, Jack shrugged his shoulders. "I don't make this shit up," he said as he fished out another smoke and lit it.

Jimmy put down his coffee. "Hey – I remember an article in the paper about a fella named... Nick Tesla demonstrating some electrical devices near the Park. The picture in the paper showed this guy-." Jimmy pointed at the picture of Frauhafer. "They looked chummy."

"Really?" Blake said. "Nikola Tesla and Frauhafer? How curious."

"Who the hell's Nikola Tesla?" Jack asked.

"A genius with electricity. He is said to have even made a boat that he can control from the shore but isn't connected by any wires. Some sort of remote device to power and move it about," Blake told Jack. "I read that the Egyptians had used the pyramids and the monoliths to create a strong electrical field that – some speculate – opened a doorway into what they called the land of the dead. I find it hard to believe, but I did hear that Tesla did an experiment with similar shapes as those in Egypt, made of the same materials, and he produced an electric radio wave."

"Where the hell did you read that?" Jimmy challenged. "Wasn't in any newspaper I read."

"I attend conferences and such. Lots of odd tidbits to be had there, books and lectures I mean," Blake stated.

"So?" Jack was annoyed at the line the conversation had taken.

"Maybe nothing. But, humans – in fact, all matter, is made up of energy. A man I met – a Werner Heisenberg told me that if one could shift the frequency of a person's particular energy, that they could phase through solid matter."

Jack took a long drag from his cigarette. "Come on, Doc, pretend I don't understand what the hell you're talking about. What exactly are you suggesting?"

Blake looked deep in thought as he puffed on his cigar. "Perhaps Frauhafer was exploring the same concept with the Government, and Tesla? Imagine if you had soldiers that could phase – and bullets would pass right through them. Or, you could phase and move through the walls of a building." He smiled. "Maybe that's what ghosts are – a person that has passed from our frequency of reality and dwells beyond our understanding."

"Back to ghosts," Jack complained. "Look – Jody Dobbs is gone. No ghost or phased person took him. Anyway – things have gone beyond just the scope of Jody Dobbs. Now I want to know who the fuck has been dogging my heels. I want to know why a factory in Pennsylvania might be involved. And, I want to know what the hell Doctor Frauhafer has to do with it all. And maybe – just maybe – I'll also get to the bottom of the misplaced Mister Dobbs!" He stubbed out his cigarette and stood up – collected all the papers and stuffed them back into his satchel. "If you're just going to paint me fiction – to hell with you all. I'm going back to my seat."

"Well – huffy," Brenda said.

Jimmy watched Jack but said, not a word. Blake looked offended, then shrugged.

"No need to get testy, Agent Parlance," Blake said more to himself than Jack.

Jack exited through the connecting door. He was passing the sleeping compartments when a hand reached out and pulled him in.

"Don't say anything," the man in a black fedora said. "My code name is Cardinal. Just listen."

Jack stood silent.

"You're heading to the MMPP. Keep your wits – they'll kill you in a second and dump your body into the machine. We've lost several agents in there. The man you know as Flannery tipped off my section at the War Department about some unsavory things going on in France. We've been following Frauhafer ever since. There is some connection between MMPP and Frauhafer – and now the Department thinks it involves one of our assets – Mister Tesla. The man is brilliant – and we are concerned that he found a way to open a doorway between our world and another."

"You're barking mad," Jack said.

"Not at all. Listen to me – I'll be watching, but when you enter the factory, I can't help you there. Take this piece of paper, and if you feel threatened while at the MMPP, hold it up. They will allow you to leave without killing you. Do not take any of your confederates in! They will not leave there alive." Cardinal stuffed the paper into Jack's satchel. "I believe that Frauhafer has been providing the MMPP with bodies for years. The products from MMPP find their way to a warehouse in New York, and from there, an entity called Mouia sees it gets sent back to his home – a place none of us want to find ourselves in. How he and his kind got here is still a mystery, but I think Tesla has figured it out. Frauhafer is trying to duplicate the effect.

"A year ago, Frauhafer built some sort of machine – and it's at his home inside Grey Manor. If the man you seek is there – he probably isn't human any longer. I hope he wasn't taken there."

The Cardinal looked out the door down the aisleway. "You're in the middle of a touchy shit-storm, my friend. Good luck." He stepped out and was gone.

Jack stood there, looking at the doorway. Stepping out, he looked up and down the walkway. No one was there. A lady came through the far door and began heading toward him, passing into the dining car. Jack went back to his seat in the coach.

A few minutes later, Blake showed up. He pulled out a flask and offered it to Jack. Jack took it and downed about half, then handed it back.

"All this nonsense is getting to my nerves," Jack said.

Blake nodded. "I understand. Seems pretty frustrating – with all the weird people, sadists, monsters, ghosts, and madmen you have to contend with." He pulled out a cigar and handed it to Jack. "Here, this will help calm your nerves." Looking at his pocket watch, Blake announced, "Only six more hours to go."

Jack put the cigar into his mouth. The acrid smoke spewed out into the car, and he seemed to relax a bit. "When we get to the MMPP location, I want you and the others to snoop around the town while I go to the factory. See if you can find any information about a cult, murders, missing people, or strange occurrences."

Blake nodded. "Not complicated. We can do it."

"Remember – don't venture near the factory, and keep safe," Jack added.

"Noted," Blake reassured Jack.

CHAPTER 16
BEYOND THE EDGE

The clack of the wheels was hypnotic. Jack felt like he'd spent half his life traveling on the rails. On every occasion, he felt the dull and charming lull of the rail sounds - a calming and sleep-inducing noise.

Looking across the aisle, he noted Jimmy and Brenda fast asleep. He straightened his gaze to the man opposite. Blake was reading a book, and at times, thumbing through a notepad he had on his lap and making notations.

Jack took out a Black Cat and lit it. "What are you reading, Doc?"

"Nelson Bucket's book on high-frequency electrical power and the warpage of space-time. Some consider it science fiction, and others think he's writing about mysterious events that have happened in New York at Shoreham Long Island," Blake said. "In his book, he claims to have seen a squid-like tentacle emerge from a ripple in the concrete floor of the room. He claimed to have suffered a terrible headache and was being rendered blind when Tesla took an ax and smashed the device. All that was left was a stench like a tide pool."

"What's at Shoreham?" Jack asked.

"Tesla's laboratories," Blake stated.

"Ah – back to this Tesla fellow. His name keeps coming up." Jack spewed smoke towards the ceiling.

Blake sat forward. "In Flannery's journal, before he begins to truly go insane, he writes that a scientist, code named Hermit, was brought in and tasked with creating a machine that can phase a person from one reality to another. He calls it the land of the dead in his journal. This scientist was, according to Flannery, a German or Pole. Could have been Tesla."

"I read Flannery's journal. Seemed like a lot of nonsense. The ravings of an insane mind." Jack expressed.

"Here, Flannery begins to babble about a

distortion in the room. Then he describes his mind splitting. Two days pass before he writes again. This time, his handwriting is shaky. He mentions that someone destroyed the electrical equipment in the room. The headache he says was gone." Blake took out the stub of his cigar and lit it. "I don't mind saying this is all very intriguing!"

Jack sat back and looked up at the ceiling as he exhaled a line of gray smoke. "Could it be that Jody Dobbs was pulled through such a distortion?"

"Unknown. This could all just be the ramblings of a mad man. But, if there was some portal opened, it is possible. Yet, I think it unlikely. So far, based on your investigation, there is no evidence that Dobbs is involved in any of this," Blake said.

"That does bother me. The link between Dobbs and any of this is scant," Jack stated. "But there is something nefarious going on, and I'm going to get to the bottom of it!"

* * *

Jack was on the frontline. His captain was missing half his head, the blood was spurting up through the jagged missing section. The man's one intact eye moved to look at Jack with terror - pleading – yet Jack could not help the man. He was going to die, and there was absolutely nothing he could do about it.

The train blew its whistle. Jack was jolted awake. The conductor came through, stating they were twenty minutes out from Williamsport. The day was growing into the late afternoon, and the sky showed the threat of rain.

They passed a crossroad. In the distance, a flash of brilliant light filled the sky. Jack jerked as the thunderclap erupted. Blake noticed his movement.

"You were in the war?" Blake asked.

"Yes," Jack replied. "It haunts me to this day."

Blake said nothing but nodded his head in

understanding.

Jimmy opened his eyes and reached over and shook Brenda. "Wakie-wakie," he said.

Brenda slapped his hand away. "Are we there?"

"Almost," Jimmy said as he rubbed the sleep from his eyes.

"About ten minutes to the station," Blake said.

Jimmy looked at his wristwatch. "Not bad – nearly 2:00 p.m."

"Enough time to catch the northbound train to Renovo," Jack said.

"This place is out in the sticks," Jimmy stated.

"Hope there's a good hotel there, and restaurant," Brenda announced.

The train cars clacked and shook as the locomotive came to a halt and blew off its excess steam. Jack and his companions made their way to the exit and out onto the platform.

There were three red-brick buildings – two that were multistory. The station attendant was directing the porters as they unloaded and loaded luggage before the giant mechanical beast headed west.

"Can you tell me when the train to Renovo will be here?" Jack asked the attendant.

The man was in his thirties, though he had white intermixed in his black beard. He looked at his watch, then up at Jack. "Fifty-three minutes. Three passenger cars and twenty boxes on this run," he said.

"Anyplace you recommend for a quick bite?" Jack furthered.

"Dolly's Place just down the street," the attendant told Jack. "Can't miss it – she's got a red-white candy-striped sign hanging down. Best steak and eggs this side the Mississippi."

They grabbed their luggage and headed off of the station boardwalk and onto the cobbled street. Not far was the striped sign.

Once inside, they ordered and discussed the next step. Jack took out his pack of smokes while Jimmy and Brenda had coffee with cream – which they both added liquor from a flask Jimmy had.

The waitress came by, and Blake stopped her. "Ever been up to Renovo?"

"Renovo?" the girl almost laughed. "Not many go that way these days. I was up there two years ago. Really just a railroad hub, small town, and some farms. Ask the station clerk there for his ghost story," she said with a chuckle. "Damn, put the frighteners on me while I was there."

Blake smiled and nodded. "Know anything about the Mercantile Meat Processing Plant?"

Her face hardened. "Locals say that people go there to work, and don't come back." She walked away toward the kitchen.

They ate a late lunch and headed back to the station. The Renovo train was coming in. It rattled to a halt, and the conductor got off. Half-a-dozen people were waiting.

"Anyone for Renovo, Bradford, or Buffalo?" he shouted.

Jack called out, and the conductor got two porters to come and get their luggage.

"Two hours to Renovo," the conductor told the group. "Three hours to Bradford, and four to Buffalo."

They boarded the train and found seats in the main coach. A half-hour passed as the engineer and his mate checked and oiled the locomotive's rods and gears. Once filled with water, the engineer gave two stout blasts from the whistle, and the train began moving.

Farmland and forests bordered the tracks. The going was reasonably straight, and only once did the train have to stop for a large herd of cattle on the tracks.

As the train came into the station, Jack checked his watch - 5:35 p.m. The passengers were let off by the stations, the train then took on a few more passengers and headed north. Jack and his companions headed into the town to find a hotel.

The Burkhalter Inn was open and accepting patrons. The air was turning chilly. Jack and his friends signed the register, then sat in the parlor with coffee, waiting for the hotel dinner.

A young boy wearing a bellhop uniform came by. "Sir, you wanted to know if we had a phone line? We have two that connect to the town switch. They can get you a line out of Buffalo to wherever you want." Jack gave the kid a quarter.

"Gee, thanks, mister!" the kid said with glee.

"Wait a minute," Jack said. "What time does the train station open?"

"6:00 a.m., sir. The station master's name is Mister Peck. He's been around these parts for a long time. He's one old fell'a."

Jack nodded. "And the sheriff? Where's his office?"

"Put up in the courthouse at the end of the street. Daniel Gammer is his name. Came back from France, and they made him sheriff around here." The kid adjusted his round cap. "Anything else? I know lots of folks in town."

Jack shook his head. "Good enough for now. Thanks for the info on the phones."

After dinner, Jack and the others went to the local bar. Out front, sitting on a bench, were two good-old-boys drinking shine from jelly jars. Just beyond the doors, bluegrass music was being played. Looked to Jack like Prohibition was not regarded much around these parts.

Jack asked a few people about Jody Dobbs. No one knew him or heard of him. By the time his watch showed 11:20 p.m. Jack was in his room and settled into the bed.

His sleep was unsettled. Several times he dreamt of a woman screaming on the tracks – then a ghostly white train ran over her. Each time, he woke with a start and struggled to get back to sleep.

By six, he was up and out the door. He made his way to the station and found the old master.

"How can I help you?" the old man asked.

"Are you familiar with the Mercantile Meat Processing Plant?" Jack asked.

"The MMPP? They have been on this line since the State's War. In 1863 the Union laid tracks going north, east, south, and west from here. We were a real hub of traffic in those days. The MMPP used to supply the troops via this very station. Then they closed the line."

CHAPTER 17
THEY STILL DWELL

"Devlin Peck is my name," the old man said, offering his hand. "Care for a cup of mud?"

Jack smiled. "Sure, I can do with some coffee."

Devlin handed Jack a blue enameled metal cup with coffee in it.

"Closed the line? The MMPP doesn't use this railway anymore?" Jack asked.

"The other way around. The railroad done quit the line that was serving the MMPP. Bring your drink and come with me." Devlin held the door open for Jack, then led him along the platform and down some stairs. They crossed the tracks heading toward the far part of the yard. "Mind the trains. I don't expect any right now – but ya gotta be on your guard at all times in a yard."

They followed some rusty old tracks from a junction lever to the start of the forest. Devlin stopped and stared out into the woods.

"Up that spur?" He looked up along the unkempt rail line. "No one goes up there."

"Why?" Jack asked.

"Back in ot-one, the old Ninety-Eight used to bring MMPP cargo through there. One day, as she was about a half-hour out, she hit a woman that wandered on the tracks. Marylou Cargrave – one of the most beautiful women in the county. She was young – twenty-three, I think – blush cheeks, ruby lips, blonde hair down to her hips."

"She was killed?" Jack put a Black Cat into his mouth and lit it.

"All her beauty was gone. Her skin was like a sack filled with broken eggshells. The impact from the train done knocked her out of her shoes and threw her corpse into the woods."

Jack took a drag, then exhaled. "So, that's why they

stopped using that line?"

"No, sir," Devlin replied. "A few months later, the old Ninety-Eight was taking a load up the line. About ten minutes out, a tremendous blast was heard. There weren't no automobiles in those days, so a group gathered up some tools and a buckboard and headed up along the road that paralleled the tracks.

"What they reported chills my bones just to think of it. They said that when they arrived up the tracks, they saw the wreckage of the Ninety-Eight. The boiler had exploded, setting fire to some of the surrounding trees and bushes. They found the crew nearby. They'd been scalded– and their skin was hanging down around their bones, and Charly Harper's body was found a hundred yards away draped over a tree limb. The engineer, Tom Hadley's face was nearly torn way, and only a rictus grin of his exposed jaw and teeth were left – his eyes had melted out of their socket."

"Then, they closed the spur?" Jack asked.

Not because of that. What caused them to close the line was…" Devlin looked up the feral tracks then back at Jack. "They saw Marylou standing on the tracks up from the wrecked train. They said she was as pale as wood ash. She smiled at them with a malevolent grin, then began walking toward the rescue crew. They turned their horses and wagon around and raced back to town. That day, they pulled up the tracks leading out of town along that line – and left the old Ninety-Eight to rust. No one's been up there as long as I've been here. The MMPP complained, but eventually laid some track going north-west, and connected with the Pennsylvania lines out by Coudersport."

Jack flicked the butt of his cigarette onto the white gravel along the tracks. "So, they tore up the tracks because of a ghost?"

"Yes, sir!" the old man said. "Over the years, the curious have gone up there. A few were driven mad, and others told of being watched from the woods. They found one fella – all his bones were crushed."

Jack walked up along the old track-bed. Several rails were gone. The steel rails beyond were rusted and unused, and the ties were splintered and rotted in places. The trees and brush up that path were wild and encroached upon the old spur. A sudden chill swept over Jack.

"Jack," called a faint voice. "We're waiting."

In the distance, Jack was sure he heard machine gunfire. He turned. "Thanks for the information," Jack stated.

"My pleasure," Devlin replied. "My advice is that you don't go up there. She's waiting on those tracks – I can feel it in me bones."

"How far is the MMPP factory up that line?" Jack asked.

"Bout ten miles to the main complex along the tracks. If you take the road, it's a two-hour drive. Don't bother going there, though. I've known plenty of folks to head up there for work. I ain't seen none ever come back." Devlin smiled a toothless grin.

"Thanks for the warning," Jack said and headed back to the hotel.

Jack found Brenda, Jimmy, and Blake in the dining room. The room smelled of fried bacon and eggs, and on the table was a stack of fried scrapple (cornmeal, pork, steak-fat, scraps of bacon, beef scraps, and goose meat formed into a loaf, sliced and fired), cups of coffee, and a pile of donuts.

"How'd you sleep?" Brenda asked.

"Same as always," Jack said, reaching for a cup of the hot java. "While I'm at the factory, go around town and see what you can find out about the MMPP and any strange occurrences associated with it."

"Will do," Blake said.

Jack turned and headed out. "If I'm not back by this

afternoon, head back to New York as fast as you can," Jack said over his shoulder.

He walked down to the sheriff's office and introduced himself, then used their phone. After talking with his H.Q., Jack asked about a ride to the MMPP site.

"Ain't none of us going up there," a deputy said. "But I think Maxwell Harford is in town. He has a farm up there. Comes into town for supplies now and again. He's over at the general store." The deputy led the way into the street and over to the store.

"Hi ya, Max," the deputy said as he came up to a man half as tall as Jack but as stout. "This here is Jack Parlance from Washington, D.C. He needs a lift up to the old MMPP plant by your farm. Can you drop him near there?"

Max looked Jack up and down, then nodded. "Sure, heading up there now. Come on."

The model T truck rattled along the dirt road heading north. At times, and on the flats, the vehicle could get up to thirty-five miles an hour.

"Why you want to go up to the MMPP?" Max asked.

"Routine visit," Jack said.

"They take my dead. Seem real eager to do so too. They send their truck around all the farms for whatever dropped dead on the ranches – in the pastures and such," Max told him.

"Sounds unpleasant. You have lots dying on your farm?" Jack asked.

"Some. Odd lights come from time to time. I find a cow or pig cut up just lying there. They seem to know when to come by. But I know 'nuf to stay clear of that place. My daddy warned me of it. He said, those brought up by the trains never leave – and none know what happen' to 'em."

"Did you ever report it to the law?" Jack put a Black Cat into his mouth.

"None of my business. I don't mind them taking the dead from my farm. Help me not have to dig a grave – you know." Max drove around a rut, then geared down for a hill. The truck slowed to fifteen miles an hour as it groaned up the rutted dirt road.

Jack smoked and watched the countryside. Trees, ranches, and farms. Occasionally they'd pass a shack or sharecropper house. He saw several barns just off the road, and windmills churning – drawing up water from deep wells.

By 10:00 a.m., they'd reached Cross Fork and the Hartford farm's access road.

"This is as far as I can take ya. There's a road two miles up that leads to the MMPP. My home is up this road here. If you need to find me, that's where I'll be." Max let Jack get out, then he throttled up, shifted the gears, and the Ford rattled up the Hartford's farm road.

Jack walked the two miles to a sign that read, 'Mercantile Meat Processing Plant, Inc.' The road was paved in cement with ditches along the edges. In the distance, he saw columns of dark black smoke rising into the sky. He began walking in that direction, tossing his butts along the roadside.

After about ten minutes of walking, a convoy of trucks approached. Jack stepped to the side as they passed without stopping. The drivers stared straight ahead – and all looked oddly similar.

Ten minutes later, Jack saw a guard post with a crossing arm. Two men with Thompsons stood at the ready.

"Hey! Who are you, and what do you want?" shouted one.

"My name is Jack Parlance. I'm from Washington, D.C., and I've come to see the plant."

The two men laughed. "Another fella from the capitol," one said to the other. "Well, come on in. I'll phone your arrival to the head office."

They lifted the arm, and Jack was allowed entrance. He heard them chuckling as he passed. "Another to feed old

Bessy."

The factory was giant. A dozen tall brick smokestacks rose a hundred feet into the sky. Many buildings littered the area, some small like tool sheds, and some five-story behemoths half red brick and the other half black-iron frames holding broad windows.

All around the ground was paved with cement or stones. Beyond, putrid black dirt lay churned up in heaps or furrows stretching to a perimeter of thick woods.

He approached a walkway – tall black iron columns on each side held up a steeply angled tin roof. The end dumped Jack out at the base of a set of steps that led up to brass-strapped double doors. And standing there was a tall thin man with a clipboard.

CHAPTER 18
CAPITAL IS KING

"Greetings, Mister Parlance from the capitol – yes?" the man addressed Jack. "You come with lots of questions, no doubt – yes?"

"I have some questions for you," Jack said.

"Good – good. We shall make straight away to my office – yes? There we shall begin the asking and the answering - yes?"

"Yes?" Jack repeated.

"Good – good. Come with me, and I will lead you there."

"Your name?" Jack asked.

"Of course – my name… what is it? I am Adolf Laborbind, the chief of accounting here – yes? For official records, no doubt – yes?"

Jack was trying to hide his irritation. "Yes," he replied.

"Come – come – we have much to impart, and you have limited time as we all do," Laborbind stated, opening the front door and waiting for Jack.

They walked along an iron-plated floor. The ground was vibrating, and everywhere Jack looked were people wandering – the thousand-yard stares fixed at some unseen horizon.

The room was large – two stories tall with wooden beams supporting a tin roof. They came to a Victorian metal archway, through a tunnel of brick, and along a path with archways open along the walls every twenty paces.

When they emerged, Jack was dazzled by the bright sunlight streaming in from the many skylights. All around were tables, and at one end, a stage with red-velvet curtains. Hundreds of people were seated – their clothes were torn, and dirty faces equally dirty. They appeared to be eating from small tin trays filled with some white viscous gelatin. Suddenly there was a horn blast, and the curtain came up with a whoosh.

A band began to play – the music off-key, and the players -- human-looking automatons – spitting sparks. A few appeared to be broken with limp limbs jittering back and forth.

"Work is good – work is great
We thank our masters for our plate
We love our work that we do
To say other is to be cold and blue
So, sing with me as I declare
MMPP is the great and fair."

Suddenly in unison, all the seated people shot to their feet, put their hands over their hearts, and began to repeat the song. Jack was stunned. His cigarette hung down on his lip as he watched. When the smoke fell to the floor, he looked over to Laborbind and saw the man watching him closely.

"See – our workers love their work – they do – yes?"

Jack nodded, then his wits kicked in, and he felt for the paper that The Cardinal had given him – he pulled out his pack of Black Cats and put one in his mouth. He lit it. "Come on – let's get on with this," he said.

Laborbind smiled, and Jack saw his mouth curve back further than it should have. A chill ran up his spine, but he followed the man into another dark tunnel.

"The machine is never stopping – churn – churn – churn – it goes. We always produce, and you can keep fighting – yes?" Laborbind said.

"Yes," Jack replied. "Fighting? What war?"

"The war – the fight between your people – the one you need food for – and we love the food too! And why not – it is mutual – you get to war; we get to enjoy – why not – yes?"

They came out into a two-story hallway. Two chained wolves the size of black bears stood watching them as they passed. The light was coming in from a set of high windows. Dust was suspended – drifting all around. The smell of age was heavy.

At the end of the hall were two doors. One was tall and made of metal – scrolling of gold and silver all over it. A plaque of gold read, 'Vladimir Peebles, Executive Officer'.

The second door was much smaller – made of painted wood. Laborbind opened the second door and went in.

Jack stepped into a room filled with books and several desks. Quill-pens ink-pens, jars of ink, and inkwells were all around. A child was huddled at one desk, his hand maneuvering a pen moving along the columns of a tally-sheet.

Laborbind sat at the most enormous desk and pointed to a wooden chair in front. He turned to a stuffed falcon on a perch next to his desk.

"Tyrel hungry – yes?" Laborbind asked, then lifted a slice of cheese from a cutting board on his desk to the beak of the bird. "Num-num-num – good Tyrel – yes?"

Jack's skin was crawling. He was far from any help. The Cardinal told him as much. His hand went into his pocket and felt for the paper, then reached into his coat and felt for the 45. All were where they should be.

"Now – why have you come – why have you come here today? We don't expect anyone from the capitol – but here you are – yes?"

"I'm looking for a missing person named Jody Dobbs? Have you heard of him or seen him?" Jack asked

"No – no Dobbs among the workers. They work, and I know them who works – there is no Dobbs here. Why else are you here? Perhaps you are here to say the contract is no more – maybe you here to see that the machine is stopped – yes?" Laborbind's voice was different. His manner like a cat toying with a mouse.

"No," Jack said. "I've come for answers." Jack took a drag from his cigarette and blew out the smoke. "What is an FSB?"

Laborbind nodded. "Yes – the Fucking Savage Beating – is a service we can provide, yes? Not our words – your words. We are sensitive to customer's needs – truly whatever they need – yes? Lots of requests these days by those near and far. We can send a contractor to fix what you need fixing – yes – not costly – not costly at all. Smash-smash here - broken there, burned, skinned. Whatever is needed."

Jack popped another cigarette into his mouth and lit it. As he did, he looked down at the planks of the wooden floor and noted other cigarette butts – old, dirty, and dusty. "Have you heard of a man named Tesla?"

"Tesla? You know Tesla – he sends the parts for the machine, the things we need, he and the government sends on the train. Is that why you have come – because of the parts? Is it that what you seek – yes?" Laborbind turned to the stuffed falcon again. He offered it more cheese, then turned back. "Where are my manners – lost for sure – yes?" He produced a crystal glass and fetched a decanter from one of the shelves. He brought it back and poured the amber liquid to the top of the glass, and a bit over the side. "Drink – drink, and we're all friends here. No one is going to the machine today – we have endless supplies to put into it – more to churn out – more – more – more come on the trains and trucks!"

"Frauhafer," Jack said.

Laborbind shot up from his chair and screamed suddenly. "You do not come here for him! He is not welcome here anymore! But, he came, and he slipped out – into the woods. He will be found – the Mouia watched him for us now, and we will have it all rectified. That is why you've come? I know now why you've come – it is because of Frauhafer – yes?"

Jack was startled -but he kept his cool. "Yes – what about Frauhafer?"

"You know – that is why you're here! He came following – seeking the machine made by the Tesla and the Mouia – but in the telegraph, the white-hats said he was not sent to us and was tricking us. We tricked him into seeing the machine – and yet somehow, he made it to the

127

forest – to the woods! Yes – yes – yes?" Laborbind grabbed the glass and threw it at the child who ducked. The glass broke, and the child immediately began to clean it up.

"The Frauhafer came to find the path of the Mouia and see the machine - he seeks the vortex – but we're sure he perished in the woods… but he was not fed to the machine, or our wolves, or the parallax." He leered at Jack. "But, now – it is hungry – the machine needs to be fed – and since there is no Frauhafer – yes? There is you!" Laborbind pulled a gold cord by his desk. A moment later, his door opened, and there stood two men with guns. "Take this man to feed the machine."

"Yes, sir!" one of the gunmen said.

Jack shot to his feet and put his back against one of the overflowing bookshelves. He first pulled out his 45, then the paper, and held both out in front of him.

Laborbind recoiled. "You – you are – you are an investor? Yes?"

Jack turned the paper and saw it was one share of MMPP. "I am!" Jack stated.

"No – you cannot be sent to the machine – you are one of the many – the investors – no, no, no – you must go – you have seen your money at work! Go back to that place you call home – and remember – buy, buy, buy more shares. The shareholders' meeting is on the twenty-first of March in New York – that place for such depravity. Bring your whip," Laborbind said. "We will not supply them."

The men at the door lowered their weapons and holstered them.

"Show the Jack out – and see he is sent on his way with care – yes?" Laborbind told the gunmen.

"This way, sir. So glad you came to visit. Anything we can do to make your visit better, please don't hesitate to ask," said one of the men. "This way, sir – we will see that you get back on your way safely."

Jack followed the guards through the warren of tunnels

and out into the smoky sunlight. They took him along a path to what appeared to be warehouses and a rail-spur.

"Now – you go – don't come back unless you're invited," One of the guards said. "Stay off the road, or you will be picked up and mistakenly processed. Just follow the tracks."

They turned and left. Jack holstered his pistol and crammed the MMPP share back into his pocket. He walked around and found the rusted rails of an old spur. It was leading south – he began walking.

Twenty minutes into his efforts, he saw an abandoned handcar. It, too, was rusted. Oddly enough, when he climbed atop it, the parts looked well-greased and oiled. He gripped the handle and pulled up with all his strength. The car began to move along the track.

Two-three pumps got the rig up to speed.

"Hey! That's my cart! Come back here with it. That's company property!"

Jack looked over his shoulder and saw a man in striped overalls shouting. The breeze was building in his ears as he drove down on the handle and pulled up. Ten miles wasn't too far. At this pace – he'd back at Renovo before the afternoon.

CHAPTER 19
LURKING FROM SHADOWS

Jack checked his watch – 12:01 p.m. He shoved down and pulled up on the lever as the handcar clacked along. There was a curve up ahead, and as he rounded it, a massive pile of twisted metal appeared.

He let go of the pump and grabbed the hand-break – but it was clear he wasn't going to stop in time – so he threw himself into the brush.

Jack tried to roll, but he hit a sapling and bumped his head on a piece of moss-covered metal debris.

The handcar smashed into the remains of the locomotive and bounced off the tracks into the woods. Jack pulled himself up to his feet and stood with his legs quivering. Reaching up to his head, he felt the blood dripping down.

There was a sound ahead of him – a noise like the giggle of a woman. Jack staggered over toward the wreckage. The boiler of the train had been ripped asunder from within. All the iron was now rusted brown.

Again, there came a giggle from the woods. As Jack cocked his head to see where the sound was coming from – by the tracks stood a beautiful woman – as white and translucent as opaque-glass. She giggled again, then began to dance in circles.

Jack wiped the blood from his eyes. She was closer. Her face was always smiling – her eyes as black as two coal lumps. She passed through a bush growing along the track.

Stepping back – Jack noticed some other shapes in the trees. There were things there – man-like but in deep shadow. They moved within the forest but did not come out. Somewhere far off, Jack heard the sound of a mouth-harp and a violin.

He began to move south along the track. The girl did not follow – but the shadows did, at least for a while.

By the time Jack came out at the rail station in Renovo,

the blood on his head had dried.

He looked at his watch at 1:15 p.m. He sought out Blake and the others and purchased tickets to Buffalo.

"What happened to your head?" Brenda asked.

"I tripped in the woods," Jack told them all. "Come on – we've got to get the hell out of here and across to Maine. It all points to Frauhafer now."

Once they got to Buffalo, they purchased tickets to Augusta, Maine. The haul would be long, and Jack explained what he thought was going on along the way.

"The MMPP is a front for some sort of smuggling. Still not sure what. Frauhafer – whatever his mad plans are – he followed a person called the Mouia to the MMPP, thinking he'd get some information regarding a machine they have.

"He almost lost his life there. He must have found out that Tesla provided some sort of electrical parts for the factory, or this mysterious machine – and made some deal to get similar machinery. The machinery is at Frauhafer's place in Maine. That's where we have to go to get to the bottom of this whole thing."

"What about Dobbs? What about the men in white hats?" Brenda asked.

"Dobbs might have been duped into financing Frauhafer – or maybe was kidnaped to extort money from his father. Still working on that part," Jack said. "The guys in the straw hats – they're evidently with the government."

Brenda shook her head. "Hell of a mess we're in."

They ate dinner in the dining car. The sun vanished behind brooding dark clouds, and the rain slammed against the windows of the train. The drone of the wheels vibrated with a rhythmic tone, and Jack was growing weary.

"The conductor rustled me up a couple of bottles. Anyone interested in a nightcap?" Blake asked.

Jack was bone tired. "Not tonight. I'm shagged – beat from all this. I need to hit the sheets." He got up and looked down at his companions. "Watch yourselves, he warned. There is no telling who might be on this train and out to stop us." Jack turned and headed to the sleeping car.

Brenda watched Jack go. "Poor sap?" she said. "I'll join you for a drink, Doc."

Jimmy finished his cigarette and stubbed it out. "What the hell – let's tie one on."

Timmy Holloway was sitting on a raised wooden log along the side of the trench. His sparkling blue eyes were visible in the low light of the breaking dawn. He was looking right at Jack.

"What a fucking mess," Timmy said. "Got a smoke?"

Jack reached into his blouse pocket and produced a pack of Lucky Strikes and tapped two out. He put one into his mouth and handed the other to Timmy.

They smoked in silence for a few minutes. Then the sunlight cut across the trench, filling it with dull warm orange light.

"You know, Jack?" Timmy asked. "When I'm killed a few minutes from now, I'll see Istanu – and I will be judged. I live in another place – born into a world without fear, or pain, or longing. I don't need to eat, drink, or even breath – but I still live. And you will too. Remember – when your mind is rattled, fire into the sparks – there you will achieve your goal."

A whistle blew. A commotion all around Jack erupted as young men he knew – dressed in the doughboy's brown lined up at the ladders. The whistle blew again, and they filed up and onto the broken ground of the killing fields. Timmy stood and put his hand on Jack's shoulder.

"Time to die," Timmy said and climbed up and over the lip of the trench.

The machine-gun fire was instantaneous. Screams carried in the air – the cries of men for their mothers - the begging to God to end their suffering. A cacophony of shouts, small arms fire, and then incoming artillery.

Sitting bolt-upright, Jack was in a cold sweat. He climbed down from the bunk and steadied himself. The car was passing a crossroad – and Jack saw illuminated by the electric light of a black Hudson with mirrored windows the roadside.

He shook his head – the crossing was gone, and they were passing tree-covered hills and far off ranches. Jack staggered out of his room and down to the lavatory and the sink. He washed his face with cold water, toweled off, and headed back to his compartment.

Jack looked at his watch – 6:25 a.m. Dressing, he took his satchel and headed to the dining car. There, he got some breakfast and black coffee.

He ate, then began pouring over his notes. One, two, three, four cigarette butts were piled in the ashtray by the time Brenda arrived.

"What you chewing over?" she asked.

Jack looked up. "Have a seat. The eggs and toast are good."

She flagged down the porter and made an order. Sitting back, she pulled out a smoke and waited for Jack to light it. "Something not settling well?"

Looking out the train window, Jack watched the checkerboard of farms going by. "I don't mind telling you that there is some queer shit happening with my case."

"Because of the strange guys who don't seem to have any blood in them and wear white straw hats? Or is it the mysterious young Dobbs who vanished without a trace? Or still, is it the cult going around killing people for some Egyptian gods? And, could it be that factory that turns dead human bodies into consumer meat products that we've all eaten?"

Jack lit up a smoke. "Sounds absurd when you put it like that."

The porter came and placed a white plate with red trim in front of her. The eggs were perfect, as were the two slices of buttered toast, and bacon. The young man poured her mug full of coffee.

"Is there anything else I can get you for now?" the porter asked.

"Not now – but don't go far," Brenda advised as she put a fin on the table as a tip.

The porter looked at the five-dollar note and smiled. "I'll be at the ready miss." He retreated toward the kitchen car.

"Look, Jack, I don't claim to know much about this world, but what I do know is that shit happens to people, and there are a lot of scary bastards out there. Jimmy's kept me safe these past few years – and I'll tell you – weirdos, perverts, con-men, huckster, yeggs, and killers are all around. If you say we got to go to Maine to find out what the hell's going on – I'm all in. I want to know what happened to the kid too. I also want to know who's going to get an ass-kicking for trying to kill me – and I'm glad you're along for the ride – G-man." She smiled at Jack.

Jack didn't smile back – his mind was a flurry of thoughts. He felt like he was over a horizon – wandering on a desolate waste with little hope of rescue.

"I'm glad you've come along," Jack said. "Look – when we get back, I'll do what I can to see you get a truckload of medicinal scotch from the federal warehouse – courtesy of Uncle Sam."

Brenda suddenly looked annoyed. "Not exactly what I had in mind – Jack." She softened. "Not too bright when it comes to women – but I think that's part of your charm." She ate her breakfast. "That town Renovo was a daffy place. Seems that place MMPP brought out all sorts of spooks and specters. Giant hungry wolves, monstrous flying men, and wandering ghosts. We got an ear full from the townies."

"Ya? I'm beginning to think there's something to all that." Jack stubbed out his cigarette and leaned back. He took out his flask and poured some liquor into his coffee.

"Porter?"

The porter came. "Sir?"

"When are we supposed to be in Augusta, Maine?"

"16 hours, sir. We have four water stops along the way to fill the Tender car." The porter stood waiting.

Jack gave the man a nickel. "Thanks." He watched the porter leave. Again, he turned to look out the window. Farmers with horses pulled scythes, waving stalks of corn, vast apple orchards, grapes cherries, potato fields. Now and then, they passed cattle ranches and sizeable white chicken coupes.

Brenda finished her plate and pushed it back. "Not bad." She took out her gold case and removed a cigarette, and waited. Jack obliged as she sat there looking at him. "Not a bad figure of a man. How'd you get that scar?"

"In the war. Artillery shell threw me into some barbed wire."

Brenda took a long drag then blew the smoke out over the table. "I take it, it was rough. I've known a few veterans. I'll forgo the usual palaver and cut to the chase – did you kill any Huns?"

"A few – some up close. There were gas and aerial shells. The machine guns were fierce. Watched a lot of men cut down." Jack stubbed out his smoke and stood. "I need to send a wireless message to my H.Q., then I'm going to the coach and relax in the lounge. You're welcome to join me."

Brenda smiled warmly. "I'll do that."

They passed Blake and Jimmy. Both looked bedraggled and hungover.

"Coffee…" Blake moaned as he passed them.

CHAPTER 20
OUT OF THE TRENCHES

The cars compressed and expanded as the line of coaches rolled into the Augusta station. After they got their luggage, Blake led the way to the ticket office. There was a train heading south and terminating in Ashdale.

Jack used the telephone and called the Ashdale police to arrange a car and possible help. Jimmy waited with the suitcases while Brenda powdered her nose.

"They said they'd loan me a car. We have to drive to Cox Head," Jack said to the others.

"Similar to when I visited in 1905 – except Frauhafer sent a horse-drawn carriage that time."

"How far is Gray Manor from Ashdale?" Jack asked.

"In 1905, it was a couple of hours – a bit of a carriage ride. Shouldn't be far by automobile – maybe forty minutes – depending on how fast we can go on the dirt road."

The conductor shouted from the small platform. "Any headed to Bath or Ashdale – all aboard!"

The porter loaded their luggage, and they climbed aboard one of two passenger coaches. The cars were old – circa 1890s – the décor was Victorian – electrically converted Pintsch gas fixtures, semi-empire design, plush wooden seats with forest green and dark red fabrics. Truly it was from a different era.

The musty smell of age was thick, and the floorboards' creaking made Jack think of the train he rode in France.

Once underway, the trip to the town of Ashdale was not long – just over an hour. They gathered their items and walked over to the police station. Jack introduced himself, and the chief showed him where the car was parked.

They stowed their items where they could, and Jack cranked the Model T Ford to life. He let out the throttle and set the gear, and away they went heading out of town. Jack looked at his watch – it was 4:19 p.m.

There were still a couple of hours of sunlight left – but the dark black clouds coming in from the coast told a tale of coming rain. All around the dark forest crouched like a hungry animal waiting to devour its prey – in there lurked fate.

They weren't far now, and Jack pulled over to the side of the road. Jimmy and he climbed out, and the gangster removed his case. Inside was a Thompson long gun with a drum magazine and several pistols. Jimmy handed the 32-caliber automatic pistol to Brenda, who tucked it into her garter.

"A girl's best friend," she quipped.

Jimmy handed the Thompson to Jack. "I'll feel better with you out front with this," he said. Jack nodded his agreement.

Blake refused to take a firearm. "It's not in my nature to use one of those," he stated.

"Okay – let's get this business out of the way," Jack said more to himself than his companions. He climbed back into the car, and they rumbled on.

There was a wooden sign that read, 'Gray Manor', and it pointed along a neatly cut road through more forest. The road was beginning to angle up.

Blake took out a half-smoked cigar and lit it. "So, Jack, what do you think was going on with that barn in Upstate – where the human figs were hanging?"

Jack adjusted the gears, and the Model T continued along the road. "

"I have no idea," Jack replied. "That thing that spoke to me – that disturbing grin…he was even less human than the one I shot."

"What do you mean less human?" Jimmy asked.

"It was as if his mouth was like a crocodile… or snake. He smiled, and the sides of his mouth stretched almost to his ears. God damn, he was unnerving."

"But – what happened when he came toward you?"

Blake asked.

"I froze… just for a moment. I couldn't move. He held some device – or maybe I was in shock. I'm not sure what happened – but I was frozen in place as was Doggerland."

"Fear can freeze a man's feet to the floor, my dad used to say," Brenda stated over the roar of the engine.

"I'd seen men suddenly stop after going over the lip of a trench – stand there as if in a trance - only to become bullet fodder for the Huns," Jack stated.

"Sounds like you were scared," Brenda said.

"Him? Don't make me laugh," Jimmy said with a huff. "That copper is too damn big to be afraid."

A mass of blond hair appeared between the professor and Jack. "My mother used to tell us about the smiler. Sometimes he's called the grinning man, or Indrid Cold. She said he'd sneak into the house at night – waited in a dark closet or under one of our beds. If we didn't behave, he'd crawl out - snapping his teeth together – before taking one of us off to where bad boys and girls go." She took a drag from her cigarette and blew the smoke into the front of the cab. "Scared the hell out of us."

"Did it keep you in line?" Jack asked.

"Sure-as-hell did! Until I became sixteen and found out what boys are good for." Brenda sat back, laughing.

Jack chuckled. "Boys? You should have been looking for a man – not a boy."

"Men and boys are often the same – especially once in bed," Brenda stated.

The road was becoming steep, and Jack geared down again. Slowing to fifteen miles an hour, the car bumped and jostled along.

After just a few miles, a light blazed out of the gloom. Jack slowed the car as the road leveled out. The smell of the cool, briny air was intense.

"An electric light," Brenda said.

"That wasn't there last I came," Blake stated.

A gatehouse came into view with two large lamps

lighting a pair of fifteen-foot high wrought iron gates. Two large cement gargoyles were perched atop the red-brick gateposts, their vacant eyes looking out down the road.

Jimmy clambered out of the back seat. He approached the tall black gates and flipped up the latch.

Jack removed a smoke, put it into his mouth, and lit it. Jimmy waved him through. Once passed, the gangster closed the gate, fixed the latch, and then walked back to the car.

"This place gives me the creeps," Jimmy said as he sat down and lit a cigarette.

Lightning flashed in the sky and was promptly followed by a clap of thunder. Jack felt the shock through the car as he drove down the road lined with tall trees.

Ahead Jack saw the outline of a large manor house. The road looped around a garden with a fountain in the middle, then led past a stable, garage, and the central portico. He pushed in the throttle and adjusted the spark arrest.

Putting the vehicle out of gear, he applied the brake and stopped at the base of the wide stairs that led to the covered entry.

Just ahead was a black Hudson – mirrored windows and the doors open. The Hudson's headlights were shining into the woods, and by the bumper, a pair of legs were protruding – wingtip shoes – spats askew.

Jimmy and Brenda got out of the car.

"Stay by the car," Jack ordered.

Brenda stood bathed in the yellow glow of the headlamps of the Model T– her golden hair draped around her shoulders. Her mouth was open with surprise. "Are those the bastards?" She produced the 32 from her pocket.

A terrifying manic laugh came from the house. It was as piercing as it was evil.

Jack stepped out of the car. In his hands was the long gun.

Blake followed.

"Stay there," Jack told Blake. Slowly Jack crept toward the legs. He saw the telltale white straw hat by the car's front wheel. Maneuvering around the open door, he stood staring down. "Doc – come here."

Blake came at once. He also looked down then knelt by the first body. Jack watched as Blake peeled back the face. The doctor drew in a rapid breath and stood again.

"Mother of God," Blake said.

"They're dead?" Jack asked.

Blake again knelt. "All I can tell you is this one has no pulse – but would it have a pulse?" He moved to the second body. "This one appears to be dead too – if they're human."

Jack came over and rifled their pockets. He retrieved two badges and two identification with pictures attached. The faces were identical in the pictures, but the names differed – Jon G. Man, and Jon H. Man. He tucked them into his pockets.

The clothes were odd – a fabric he'd never felt before. The hats weren't straw either – but made to look like straw hats.

"Most curious," Blake said.

There was a flash of lightning, a distant clap of thunder, and the rain began to fall.

The mad laughter came from the porch – something was there.

"Look!" Brenda shouted while pointing at the upstairs windows of the mansion.

Faces were looking out, then they were gone. Light emitted from several windows of the house with a bright white glow. The wind began blowing as lightning erupted again in the sky, followed by a brutal ear-shattering thunderclap.

Brenda nearly jumped from her skin, "Holy shit," she cried out. "I hope that doesn't happen again."

Doctor Blake went to the vehicle's back seat, removed the toolbox, and tucked it under his arm.

Jack reached inside his tweed coat feeling for the 45-automatic pistol, making sure it was easy to get.

Jimmy looked up at the mansion. "There's someone up there," he said. "I saw a shadow move past the window."

Jack moved up the granite stairs to the door. With the long gun cradled in the crook of his arm, he tried the door latch. The door was unlocked.

"Come on," Jack said as he pushed the door inward. He peered inside.

The stench of death flooded out the door. Jack cocked his head as if he was hit in the jaw, then turned his head back to open door.

"God! That's...awful..." Brenda stammered as she wretched a few times by the steps.

Doctor Blake followed - the box firmly held in his hands.

The room was square with a staircase in front and French doors to each side. On the hardwood floor was a lower torso and a bloody smear leading towards the left set of French doors. Jack motioned with his hand for Jimmy to stand by the door.

Congealed blood was thick and dark on the floorboards. The lower half - butt, legs, and feet - appeared to belong to a woman since the feet were wearing high heels shoes, and the torso was dressed in half a dress.

Jack placed his hand on the door handle and rocked it down, then pulled it open just a little. The smell of burnt flesh was nearly overpowering.

The soft yellow glow of an electric lamp shined on Jack's face. Inside, he saw the charred remains of the other half of the torso. Nothing around it was burned, not even the wooden floor.

Jack slipped in and put his back to the corner, the long gun raised. It was clear that the room was a lady's parlor, with sumptuous couches detailed with felt and fringe, and a round coffee table covered in doilies with a silver serving platter in the middle.

It looked to Jack that the tea set was placed, then jostled by a fight. A chair was toppled, and the table askew.

On the opposite wall, Jack saw a fire in the fireplace flickering away as if freshly fueled.

"Come on in," he said as he opened the door all the way.

"Oh, my God!" Brenda exclaimed in horror and shock.

"That's unpleasant!" Jimmy said.

"It's to be expected," Blake stated. "Horrors upon horrors, as written in the ancient text."

"Who the hell could have done this?" Jimmy asked.

"A real sick fuck!" Jack growled.

"Not who, but what," corrected Blake. "Can't you feel it in the air? A feeling building like that of a man standing at the edge of a cliff and looking over?"

From outside echoed the sharp cry of a wolf. Inside - the cackling laughter of madness blared from beyond the doorway. The parlor door slammed shut, and three of the four jumped. Jack stood stock still and listened as the wind outside began howling – then came more howling of a different sort.

"Is that a dog?" Brenda asked.

"A wolf," Jack said. "And I suspect not the ones we're used to."

"You can bet on that," Blake said. "I'm concerned there is more afoot here than even I suspected."

Jimmy opened the parlor. The room was empty, and the main door was open like they left it. "At least the doors are still open out here."

A scream of horror echoed from upstairs. Jack moved to the stairwell and raised his long gun. "Jimmy, follow me," Jack ordered.

"Not on your life!" Jimmy said as he brought up the colt and pointed it at the top of the stairs. "I'll cover you from here."

Brenda slapped Jimmy on the arm. "Don't be a coward!" she chided.

Jimmy seemed to pull himself together. "Ya – I'm not afraid," he reassured himself.

Brenda moved to close the front door. "It's raining hard outside now," she said.

Jack placed his foot on the first step but promptly moved it to the floor again. A feeling had overcome him, a sense of terror. There was something upstairs coming, and he did not want to meet it on the stairs.

A dark shape was at the top of the landing. It stood there for a moment. In the low yellow light from the electric wall sconces upstairs, Jack saw a person's outline.

"Who are you? I'm a law enforcement agent - show me your hands," Jack ordered.

Unnerving laughter - painful - angry - forced by some unimaginable force erupted from the shadow. It moved quickly, flying past Jack, Jimmy, and the doctor. The thing was on Brenda. She screamed in terror – then began laughing hysterically as it lifted her from the ground and tried to drag her toward the other set of French doors.

"Don't let it get away!" Blake shouted in panic.

Suppressing the terror, Jack rushed the attacker and leaped onto it, locking his arms around it tightly.

Brenda was now screaming with laughter as she cried out in anguish.

The figure turned its head to look into Jack's eyes – it was a chalk-white clown face – black triangle markings above and below the eyes, a red nose, and a frowning red-painted lips.

Jack wrenched it from Brenda – but in the process, he looked hard into its leering grinning face – to his horror, it was not makeup – but the natural markings of the thing.

Blake threw open his box and removed a talisman. Rushing to the creature, he thrust it above his head and loudly proclaimed something in a lyrical voice.

The creature reared back, breaking Jack's hold, and ran madly for the stairs. Jack ran after it but came back seconds later with a perplexed look.

Brenda lay on the ground spasming with uncontrollable laughter.

"It vanished," Jack said.

Brenda was catching her breath. She stopped laughing. "It…was like…" she gasped for air. "Like…a million fingers were tickling me all over!" she got out. "I think I wet my pants!"

"Dammit, Doc!" Jack swore. "What in the God damn hell was that thing?"

"Something not of this world," Blake stated flatly. "Things are entering our realm. There will be more. We will need to be on our guards even more."

There came a scream from down the hallway.

"The scream!" Jack blurted.

"No, Agent Parlance!" shouted the doctor. "They're already done for. We need to find the basement. It will lead to a subterranean chamber that leads to the sea."

CHAPTER 21
BROKEN

"How do you know this?" asked Jack.

"From when I was here last. Doctor Frauhafer took me on a tour of the underground chambers. I left the very next day."

"What was down there?" Brenda asked as she stood up.

"If I were to impart to you in all its detail, you would be dumbstruck and frozen with paralysis. Suffice to say, he was conducting experiments that should not have been attempted."

"Let's get down there then!" Jack stated boldly.

"Ya, let's run headlong to our deaths!" Jimmy said. "Wouldn't it be prudent to summon the police from Ashdale?"

Jack looked around. "I don't see a phone in here."

Jimmy looked in both parlors. "None in these rooms either."

"We're wasting time. Come on – if it's our death we go to meet – so be it," Jack stated and moved around the stairs. "After all, who the fuck wants to live forever?" Jack asked as he pulled another cigarette from his pocket and lit it. "Alright, Professor, lead the way!"

Blake took the lead. They traveled through several corridors to a long hallway with wood paneling and chair railings. Stopping halfway, he probed around on the wood floor with the toe of his shoe. A clicking sound filled the air as one of the panels popped open. Pulling open further, he motioned for Jack, Jimmy, and Brenda to follow.

Bare electric lights illuminated the corridor. The hall was narrow, just big enough for people to walk single file. At the end of the hall was a set of stairs leading down. The smell of the sea was strong, filling the air with the harsh brackish odor of stale saltwater and rotting seaweed.

Slowly they made their way down. The air was growing colder, and moisture dripped from the walls and ceiling.

"Who are you! Do you come to cross, or do you come to feed?" A distant voice called out.

Blake stopped and held up his hand with the symbol. He chanted a few odd words and turned to Jack. "That was telepathic – it was in our minds," he told them.

"Your souls I shall feed upon. Bring me your life," the voice commanded.

The great bellow of a wolf echoed. It was close. Jack kept the long gun at the ready.

Blake stopped at a stone landing. Below, the sandy ground was visible.

"Prepare," Blake said.

Stepping onto a grainy, rocky surface illuminated by bare bulbs, Blake and the others were facing a tunnel. In the distance, a chanting echoed off the stone walls. It was a rhythmic sound that was lulling and hypnotic.

"This way," Blake said softly.

Moving into a passage, they traveled a few dozen feet. Wooden doors with bars appeared. Moaning was audible from within, and Brenda stopped to look inside. The room was dark, but there was someone or something there. She saw it move, the light reflecting off some bits of clothing.

"Professor, there's someone in here!" Brenda called in a hushed voice.

"Not someone, but something," Blake replied. It would be a terrible mistake to open one of these doors."

Brenda glanced into the room again. The light showed a face, or lack of one, as it fumbled about within the cell. There were no eyes or nose - only a mouth that appeared to be overly large. The thing seemed to be human-like but was certainly not a person. Brenda looked back at the group, her eyes wide with terror.

"Maybe we should keep moving," she said, her nerves shaken.

The tunnel made a ninety-degree turn and emptied into another large chamber. A space two hundred feet round and a hundred feet high met their gaze.

The air was sickly, filled with the stale brine smell and rot. Jack took a long draw from this dwindling cigarette, then tapped the professor on the shoulder. "Now what?" he whispered.

"I'm not sure," Blake replied.

Among the chanting was a buzzing – like that from a large radio filled with faulty tubes.

Blake took out some items from his case. "I'm not sure if these will help. If Frauhafer has created a vortex, we may be in deep trouble. If you see any equipment in there – focus your attention on it – destroy it as soon as you can."

"What happens if we get separated?" Jimmy asked.

"Don't!" Blake warned.

Stepping into the room, they were confronted with a gathering of more than thirty people dressed in white robes. They were all facing a cliff where Doctor Frauhafer was standing atop.

Around the worshipers were seven slabs of cement, each with a person chained to it. The image of the Egyptian gods was on each one. Atop each table was a pole of metal.

Blue flares of electric arcs were bouncing from pillar to pillar. Machines were stationed between the cement, the faint sound of generators bubbling up from the darkness.

Frauhafer's hands were raised to the cavern roof as he chanted. The assembled chanted too, and the sound echoed off the walls masking the intruders.

The sound of the sea was barely audible. Upon the plateau next to Frauhafer, a large statue twenty feet tall lorded over those worshippers. A great beast of a man with the head of a crocodile.

Jack entered the chamber and flicked his cigarette's remains off into the pool of black water to his left. The professor slipped around in the shadows to the right.

"Shoot anyone who comes at us," Jack told Jimmy and Brenda.

For a moment, the chanting increased. The air rippled

like water. Electric arcs burst all around, dancing over the bodies of the robed figures. Above, Frauhafer was doing something with his hands. The stench of rotting flesh wafted down from above as the darkness of the cavern roof began to twist and distort.

Jack took out a cigarette and put it in the corner of his mouth.

"Should you light that – now?" Brenda whispered.

"The time for stealth is passed," Jack whispered back. He fished out his lighter. Cradling the Tommy gun in the crook of his elbow, he brought the lighter up and flicked it to life.

The chanting stopped. All those below Frauhafer turned to face Jack, Jimmy, and Brenda.

"You're all under arrest by the power invested in me by the United States Government!" Jack roared. "Throw up your hands and surrender!"

The white hooded faces looked out, all surprised. Then the surprise turned to anger.

"Oh, my God!" Jimmy said as he planted his feet wide and tightened his finger on the trigger.

"That's what I thought, too," Jack said with no emotion.

"Kill them!" shouted Frauhafer.

The worshipers came at Jack, Brenda, and Jimmy. Then the room lit up with the blaze of the Tommy gun.

Jack let loose and began mowing down the cultists as they rushed him. The bodies fell like wheat to a scythe as he swept the chopper back and forth, angling rounds into the machines in the alcoves. Fireballs burst forth, and electrical discharge blasted all those in the cavern.

A crack of thunder shattered the air and drove Jack, Brenda, and Jimmy to the ground. A great weight was now upon them, and they could not move.

Looking up, Jack saw Blake and Frauhafer struggling. Above them, a distorted vision appeared. From that darkness, a host of tentacle flew down. Two grabbed

Frauhafer and tore him in two as he screamed in pain and terror. Another two grabbed a man in a white robe and pulled him into the darkness, screaming all the while. Another reached for Blake but halted as he held up some talisman. A sound fell from the ceiling like the beating of a kettle drum inside their heads.

The creature emerged from the twisted ceiling. There was no describing it – the shape – the distortion – the smell – all caused those who looked upon it to scream in agony.

Blake screamed unknown words as he read from a scroll. The thing was receding. Tentacles touched Jack – lifeless – cold – clammy – then they snapped back into the twisted roof and were gone.

Consciousness was fading as Jack struggled to pull the Thompson up to fire it. The gun was too heavy, and then a voice in his head began to drive him mad.

Slowly, the weight on his chest was lessened, and he saw Jimmy climb to his feet and claw at his face screaming in tongues. Brenda ran into the darkness. Jack, too, was in full panic. His heart was in his throat, his limbs were moving, the walls of the cavern passing him. Those wooden cell doors were now open. There was no control – his body was in some automatic mode – no recovery – no reprieve from the pain in his head or the panic in his soul.

Jack knew the wolves were in the darkness of his mind now. They would feast upon his soul if he stopped. Sounds of grunting were right behind him – in his ear – the hot breath of an unholy beast at his heels. The rain on his face felt like acid – and the forest was breathing as the white-light of lightning cut through the clouds. Darkness descended, and he was out.

* * *

"Jack!" A loud voice shouted at him. "You've been out for some time. Do you know where you are?"

Slowly his eyes opened. Dale York, the Bureau's

psychiatrist, stood over him. In one hand was a hypo, in the other smelling sauce. "Do you remember what happened to you?

"Am I in an infirmary?" Jack asked in the dazed voice of a man half-awake.

"You're at the hospital at Bellevue. It took ten men to take you into custody."

"What happened?" Jack asked.

"We'd like you to tell us that. You stopped reporting two weeks ago. A patrolman found you wandering the streets of Brooklyn carrying a long gun and babbling incoherently."

"Blake – Jimmy, Brenda?" Jack asked as he tried to sit up. Realizing that he was strapped to the bed with leather restraints, he shook his head and looked about. "What the hell's going on!" he demanded.

"Okay, easy big fella, like I said, it took ten men just to bring you in. You were clearly out of your mind." Doctor York said. "We sure didn't want to take a chance that you might hurt one of us or yourself."

"What happened to Brenda, Jimmy, and Blake?"

"We don't know. All we know is that you were found walking around in Brooklyn. Were those people with you when you…I mean, what was the last thing you remember?"

"A tunnel or chamber underground. It was by the ocean, I think. There was this thing… a face – no – an octopus – it was killing people. Blake was… I can't remember. But I do know that Doctor Frauhafer was a murderer and kidnapper."

Flynn came into the room. "No one's heard from him since you vanished. We were hoping that you could shed some light on the issue."

"Vanished? He's dead, torn in half by…no wait, maybe that was a dream…"

"Get some rest, and we'll see how you're doing tomorrow. You're still a bit muddled. Chloral hydrate can add to that." Doctor York turned to leave.

"Doc?" Jack asked.

Stopping, York turned back. "What is it? Did you remember anything else?"

"Do you got a smoke?"

"Get some rest. You're off the cigarettes for the time being," York told Jack.

Flynn looked at York and shook his head. "Will he be okay?"

York shrugged his shoulders.

Flynn came over near Jack. "Oh – by the way, that kid, Jody Dobbs – he turned up. Turns out he was hiding out in the Virgin Islands. Took a steamer called the Maine over when he got out of the loony bin. Customs picked him up when he tried to come back into New York a few days ago."

"You're shitting me?" Jack stated.

"Really – the kid just turned up out of thin air. Get some rest. Looks like you're on the mend. Take your time – your job is here when you check out as okay." Flynn exited the room.

York looked back. "I'm going to give you a sedative. So, try and have a solid sleep." He injected Jack, then turned out the light as he left.

The room fell into darkness. Only the light from the rectangular glass window in the door came into the room from the hall.

Jack lay back. The tight white sheets were nearly suffocating. He kicked his feet a few times to loosen them.

The soft light of the moon was shining through the window and bathing the room in an unearthly glow. He saw the nurse look in as she hustled by. On the end table were his pack of Black Cats. He wanted to reach over and grab them, but the restraints wouldn't allow it.

The sedative was taking effect. He was growing drowsy. He looked at the white medicine cabinet in the room. Pills, solutions, ointments hidden behind the glass panes all lined up. Then, he noticed in the reflection in the glass doors a face that was not his own.

The face was round, the eyes spaced oddly wide, and the mouth - grinning at him with white teeth. Then, it snapped its jaws together - tick-tick-tick.

Jack's hair stood on end as his eyes went wide. The air turned frigid as his breath rushed into the room in rapid puffs of thick mist.

His heart drove hard against his ribs as he realized his eyes were closing. He struggled to keep them open as he tried to call out for help. Only a raspy rattle exited his dry lips as his eyelids slipped down. An immutable darkness came, and he was in a deep dark and dreamless sleep.

ABOUT THE AUTHOR

The author Lawrence BoarerPitchford has penned more than seven novels. He has created tales of fantasy often with dark overtones and flawed anti-heroes. Along with fantasy, he has written novels of historical fiction, and science fiction, all providing the reader with vivid settings and relatable characters sure to titillate the avid reader.

If you liked The Cox Head Horror, you may also like some of his other works. They can be found at Amazon Books.

Classic Fantasy
> **The Lantern of Dern Blackhammer**
> **In the World of Hyboria**
> **The Last Atlantian Prince**

Steampunk/SciFi
> **Harrow's Gate**
> **Jake and the Solomon Lake Treasure**

Historical Fiction
> **Sawbones**.
> **Thadius**

Horror/ Mystery/ Detective
> **The Cox Head Horror**

www.ingramcontent.com/pod-product-compliance
Lightning Source LLC
Chambersburg PA
CBHW020341260626
47156CB00004B/1633